Dedication

With love to Robert.

Chapter One

It's a Small World...Isn't it?

It was barely 10:00 A.M. and Michelene Tyner was already falling behind schedule, even though she'd valiantly made every effort to stay a step ahead of the game today. She'd gone so far as to set her alarm an hour early and put the percolator on the night before. Although she was the best at what she did, timeliness was not her strongest attribute. As a result she made use of all the technological gizmos she could get her hands on to help her cause.

Her favorite being her palm-top computer which she was now scanning. According to the information on the illuminated screen, she had three clients to see before the end of the business day, and several stops to make before she could see anyone. Pressing the print key, she impatiently tapped her Italian loafer-encased foot while her printer spit out her schedule. As much as she relied on electronics, there was nothing like a sheet of paper as backup. You could never be too careful.

Still, if she had as much sense as she always insisted she did, she'd get an assistant, as her best friend and mother hen, Lisa Renoir, had been suggesting for the past year. However, Michelene lived by the words of her now deceased mother, "no one can do what you do like you do." Words to live by. As a result, in the five years that her personal shopping service, Exclusively Yours, had been in existence, the business had grown exponentially. She'd started her business as a tribute to

1

her mother and a gift to herself on her thirtieth birthday. And she hadn't regretted one minute.

People who didn't know or understand the business thought of her profession as frivolous nonsense…shopping around the world, perusing magazines all day, visiting art galleries and car dealerships. Still Michelene insisted—no, demanded—of herself that she give each and every one of her quirky clients the personal attention for which she'd become renowned throughout New Orleans. Which, on the downside, was what took up so much of her time, as it had this morning. A perfect example was the unexpected visit of Percy Hawkins earlier.

And as much fun as it was to chat with Percy, his last-minute appearance had thrown her off. But what could she do, toss him out? One of the homegrown heroes of Algiers, Louisiana, Percy had become an NBA superstar. So much so, that to avoid being mobbed, he generally had to sneak into town. But he never missed coming to see Michelene to place some extravagant order, which he knew she would be able to fulfill.

In the midst of asking her advice on selecting the perfect gift for a "friend" of his, he had her doubling over in laughter with locker room stories. She'd actually had to gently ease him toward the door, or else they'd still be sitting on her couch chatting.

She considered herself a connoisseur of human nature and sometimes she became so absorbed in the stories, scandals, joys and heartaches of her clients that she would totally lose track of time. But they appreciated her. She was like a high-priced bartender, or hairstylist, to whom people just felt free to tell their tales. But what they didn't know was that the very things they revealed to Michelene, as she sat patiently listening and nodding her close-cropped head of curls, were mentally catalogued—all those little tidbits gaining insight into their personalities, their wants and desires, which were the keys to her success. Her intuitive ability to select the perfect item invariably astonished her customers every time. She had a knack for sensing their wants before they realized they were needs. "How do you do it?" they would always ask in amazement.

She smiled as she snatched the printout with one hand and straightened the frame that held her Fine Arts degree which hung above her desk with the other. "'Cause I'm good."

Snapping the cover of the palm-top closed, she picked up her gold and black kente-covered portfolio that she always kept on the right-hand side of her desk, shoved the mini computer inside the pouch and turned on the answering machine.

Walking briskly in short-legged strides through her home office, which was an eclectic blend of living room charm and hi-tech chic, with its overstuffed bronze brushed-cotton couch and matching love seat, horseshoeing a low, smoked glass and wood coffee table, thirty-two inch Sony television and VCR, which was accompanied by a top-of-the-line computer system, scanner, printer, fax machine and three-line telephone, Michelene shut the door behind her and jogged upstairs to her bedroom.

The large peach-tone room always made her say ahh everytime she stepped across the threshold, as she did now. No matter how harried or frazzled she was, her bedroom mystically had the ability to slow her down and soothe her.

Crossing the gleaming wood floors, she retrieved her hand-sewn leather briefcase from her walk-in closet, and her cream-colored linen jacket from the padded hanger, which she duly noted went perfectly with her chocolate mousse-toned palazzo pants. Although she loved the feel of silk and the look of rayon blends, the humid Louisiana weather didn't feel the same way. During the grueling months of summer, she swathed herself in flowing cottons and linens, to allow her body to breathe. She headed out, grabbing her keys, her little remote and her cell phone.

On the way downstairs, she deactivated the car alarm with a touch of the button on the black box of her key chain. Her latest gadget was the remote, which she could use to start the car. She grinned as she heard the car hum to life out front. Her car broker and could-be boyfriend, Paul Dupre, had gotten the Benz CLK convertible for her and had all the accessories added without additional charge. Paul had even had it custom painted to a metallic bronze. The only one of its kind. He was sweet, but he was also as smooth-talking as whipped butter. That man could sell you your own soul. Half the town drove around in cars that she'd suggested, which were then purchased through Paul's network of dealers. She grinned. He was almost as good at what he did as she was. Almost.

The instant she set foot outside she got smacked square in the face with the unbelievable humidity that clung to her skin like flypaper and zapped her of breathable air. The few short steps from her front door to her driveway five feet away made her feel like running back inside and taking a shower. She couldn't get into her car fast enough. She swatted away a mosquito and practically dived into the car. The cool air wrapped around her, slipping teasingly beneath her sleeveless blouse.

"Thank heavens for technology," she muttered, settling back as her seat belt slid into place.

She checked her rearview mirror and noticed a smudge of mascara along the bottom of one wide, brown eye. Taking a tissue from the box she religiously kept in the glove compartment, she dabbed under her eye, and while she was at it, added a hint more of her berry lipstick, which Lisa said did wonders for the rich red undertones of her honey-brown skin. Checking her reflection, she agreed.

Satisfied, she slowly pulled out. Image may not be everything but it was a helluva lot. It was the foundation of her business, and she was her business. How she looked, presented herself, was a direct reflection of what she could do for her clients. And by the time she got finished with them, they felt the same way about themselves. Just as she was sure her newest client, Lance DuBois, was beginning to feel.

Michelene had been working with the high-priced attorney for the past three months and the transition was nothing less than a miracle. Introduced to him at a charity event, she'd immediately assessed his total lack of what worked for him

4

and took him under her wing. Now, Lance had been trans-
formed from a back cover to a front cover, a fitting tribute to
one of the owners of the leading black law firm in New
Orleans.

She peered at the digital clock on the dash, quickly compared it to her gold bracelet watch—a little something she'd
picked up last Christmas when she'd gone to Cartier's in New
York—and groaned. Her fleeting hope that the digital was
wrong just evaporated. She had fifteen minutes to make the
half-hour drive. Reaching for her cell phone, she pressed the
two-digit speed dial number for DuBois, Merchant and—most
recently—Alexander, and stepped on the gas.

Living outside of the city proper of New Orleans had its
benefits. She had privacy, was surrounded by lush land, water
and wildlife, all the things she loved. Her neighbors were far
enough away as to be unobtrusive, but close enough in the
event of an emergency. And the seclusion of her sprawling
town house gave a hint of mystery to her business and provided her clients with absolute privacy.

Every time she thought about how lucky she was to have
gotten the house and the great deal, she could just kiss Martin
Benoit, the realtor. But then again, that's what he wanted and
more. Martin was sweet and devilishly handsome in that "creole of color" kind of way—but—well that was another story.

"DuBois, Merchant and Alexander. May I help you?"
came the slow, easy drawl.

Michelene's honeyed features brightened. She liked
Marie, the firm's very affable but totally efficient secretary.
Michelene couldn't help but admire Marie's ability to juggle
an assortment of tasks, not get frazzled and still stroll out at
five on the dot. They'd made fast friends when she'd taken on
Lance. Though she'd only visited the office two or three
times, she talked with Marie by phone often, trying to coordi-
nate Lance's schedule with hers.

"Hi, Marie. It's Michelene Tyner."

"Miki!" she bubbled, then quickly sobered. "Anytime you
give me your last name I know you're going to be late."

Michelene laughed. "That's why they pay you the big bucks, Marie. About twenty minutes," she asked more than stated. "Will Lance still be around?"

"I'll let him know." She flipped through the appointment book. "If you hurry you may catch him. He has an appointment in about an hour. The place is in chaos anyway."

Michelene frowned. "Why? What's going on—major murder case or something?" she asked, hoping to get an inside scoop, but knowing deep down she wouldn't. She knew Marie loved to talk nonstop when the moment hit her, but company business never crossed her lips.

"Nothing quite that interesting. One of the offices is being renovated and workmen are crawling all over the place."

"Oh," she sighed, disappointed again. "Well, I'll be there as soon as I can."

"See you then."

Michelene disconnected the call and slid the slim Motorola Startac cell phone into the portable charger.

Pressing the preprogrammed button on the radio, *Baby, Baby Don't Cry,* by Smokey Robinson filled the confines of the Benz from the local R&B classic station, WWOZ-FM. She stepped on the accelerator, humming along. She really didn't want to keep Lance waiting—too long, but she needed to stop by Lisa's gallery and pick up a piece she'd ordered for his office.

Michelene smiled. Lance had come a long way, baby. Not only had she been able to upgrade his wardrobe, he was now interested in art, which was fine with her. Lisa got the sale and Michelene got the commission.

She zipped down Route 46, made that sharp snake curve that she loved, doing a sweet seventy-five, pushing eighty, when she heard the wails behind her.

"Damn!" She peered into the rearview mirror and saw the distinctive swirling red and blue lights. Easing on the brakes, she pulled slowly onto the shoulder of the two-lane road and came to a stop, rolling down her window.

"Hey there, Beau," she greeted, putting on her best smile.

6

"Ms. Tyner," he drawled as he tipped his hat and leaned down, bracing his huge hands on the open window frame. He took a cursory look into the interior, languidly looked up and down the road, then zeroed his grass-green eyes on Michelene's innocent-looking face. "Going pretty fast there, Ms. Tyner."

"Was I? You know Beau, I'm late for an appointment. I guess I was so concerned about holding up my client, I just wasn't thinking about anything but getting there." She tried on her contrite look. "I sure am sorry."

"You know I need to write you up." He rubbed his stubbled chin. "The take this month at the station is dinner for two. I'm already behind Lou by ten tickets." He pulled his hat a bit lower over his brow.

She reached out and patted his hand, her voice filled with compassion. "I understand that you have a job to do there, Beau. I sure do." She blew out a breath and nodded her head in acceptance.

Beau looked up and down the lane again. "Aw hell, Cissy and me gets out enough anyhow. Never catch up to Lou no way. I'll let it go this time, Ms. Tyner. But you take it easy out here. Wouldn't want to see you and that pretty car wrapped around a tree."

"Thank you, Beau. I sure do appreciate your understanding. And I'll be sure to remind Paul about that car for your wife. I know I can find something that's perfect for Cissy and the kids to get around in."

"'Preciate that." He tapped the roof of the Benz. "Take care now, Ms. Tyner."

"I sure will, Beau. And thanks." She pressed the button and the window slowly slid upward.

Beau ambled back to his patrol car, started the engine and pulled out, waving as he passed her car. Michelene smiled and waved back.

"Whew. That wasn't so bad. Lucky for me Beau isn't as diligent at giving out tickets as Lou," she mumbled. She reached into her purse and pulled out her palm-top. *Don't for-*

get to talk to Paul about a car for Beau's wife, she typed, flipped the cover closed and pushed it back into her bag.

She took a peek in her mirror and quickly ran her fingers through her cap of curls, hoping to bring back the bounce. The few minutes of her hair being exposed to the cloying humidity was on the verge of giving her a bad hair day. Satisfied that her coif had been salvaged, she checked her sideview mirrors and eased back onto the road, making a concentrated effort to keep her speed in the general vicinity of the limit.

Once she'd gotten into the town proper, she made her pit stops, picking up the two suits that were sent to her personal tailor for alterations, stopped by The Gallery on Julia Street and picked up the piece of art she'd had specially framed, only having time to peck Lisa on the cheek and swear to her that they'd get together later. Then it was off to Hennesy's where the handmade tablecloths, placemats and napkins she'd ordered for the mayor and his wife were ready and waiting.

Finally she could get to her appointment with Lance. She checked the digital clock, compared it to her watch. Forty-five minutes late. "Damn."

Fortunately Michelene found a parking space on Charles Street only two doors down from the offices of DuBois, Merchant and Alexander.

Taking one of the boxed suits and the brown paper-wrapped art from the backseat, she juggled her purse, closed the door with a snap of her hip and hurried through the revolving door, nearly getting stuck when the suit box became momentarily wedged in the door.

She checked the box when she'd stepped free of the door. Nothing really obvious, just a slight dent in one corner. Lance would never notice. All he would see was the suit, of that she was sure. Lance was strictly a beneath-the-surface kind of guy. The packaging made no difference to him at all. That fact was painfully obvious in the wardrobe he'd chosen prior to her arrival in his life. *Ooh, be nice*, she warned herself. She adjusted the box beneath her arm, confident that the suit was in the same condition as when she'd watched the tailor pack it.

Opting for the stairs, rather than waiting for the elevator, Michelene walked up to the second-floor law offices.

The instant she cleared the landing, finding herself in the entry foyer, she saw exactly what Marie was talking about earlier. Curling her nose in distaste, Michelene tiptoed across a drop cloth, around a stack of two-by-fours, passed several workmen, careful not to brush against anything or anyone, then pushed open one of the twin glass doors.

Marie was not at the front desk and there was no one out front who didn't look like they belonged on the cover of *Construction Weekly*.

She walked down the short, carpeted corridor, just as Marie stepped out of one of the offices.

"Made it, I see," Marie greeted, closing the door behind her.

"Finally," Michelene huffed.

"Can I help you with those?"

"No. Thanks. Is Lance still here?"

"You just missed him by about ten minutes."

Michelene sucked her teeth in annoyance, a habit her mother had tried unsuccessfully to break her out of since she was eight years old. "I hope he wasn't too upset."

"No. Not at all."

"Well, here's the suit he ordered," she said indicating the box tucked under her arm, "and the picture he wanted framed. I guess I could leave him a note—"

The front desk phone rang.

"Excuse me. Let me get that call." Marie began walking. "Just drop everything off in his office and leave the note," she said over her shoulder.

"Thanks, Marie."

Michelene continued down the corridor, beyond the first closed door, passing a man clad in what were once white overalls hauling a gallon of paint, and opened the door to the second office on the right.

The instant she stepped inside the plush space, she saw her distinctive signature all over it, from the recent purchase of the ergonomically correct desk and leather chair to the John Biggers artwork that adorned the sandstone walls.

Strolling across the imported Persian rug, she deposited the box and the picture on the desktop then came around to sit in the high-back chair. Pulling the embossed notepad across the desk, she began to jot down her message for Lance.

Just as she was right in the middle of crafting her apology, the office door opened. Her gaze rose from the notepad to the figure that filled the doorway. He was fine. No question about that, even in the paint-stained jeans and a denim shirt. And she knew fine when she saw it. "Mr. DuBois is out of the office if that's who you're looking for," she said in an offhand manner before going back to her note.

"I know. I saw him when he left."

Hmm. Great voice, too. She kept her eyes on the off-white paper. "I'm sure Marie is up front, if you need something." She signed her name with a flourish and stood.

"I didn't realize the firm had hired someone new. I thought I'd met everyone."

Her eyebrow arched in suspicion. Maybe he was the head painter or something. What other reason could there be for him thinking he should be so forward? "I don't work here."

The corner of his wide mouth curved up on one side as he leaned casually against the door frame as if he had all the right in the world to be standing there, Michelene thought as she stared him down.

He folded his arms across his chest. "Oh, my mistake. You looked so comfortable in that chair, like you belonged in it," he said with a tinge too much accusation in his tone as far as Michelene was concerned.

She jutted her chin forward. "I work for Mr. DuBois. He's a client of mine." Why was she telling him this?

Michelene took her purse and sashayed back across the rug to the door.

"And what is it that you do exactly?"

She pursed her lips and looked up at him, then dug in her pocket, pulled out her business card and slipped it into the top pocket of his shirt. "Maybe you know someone who could use my services. Have a nice day."

He angled his body to the side to let her pass, but not before catching the soft scent of heaven as she did.

"You, too," he said to her back. "And that bit of plaster on your nose goes well with that outfit."

For a split second she cringed. "It's a fashion statement," she tossed back barely missing a beat and kept going.

He watched her until she turned the corridor before he pulled the card from his shirt pocket.

Embossed in gold on black followed by her phone number was *Exclusively Yours—Michelene Tyner.*

So that was Michelene. Lance hadn't stopped raving about her. He looked at the card again and smiled before slipping it back into his pocket.

The instant she turned the corner, she pulled her compact from her purse and peered at her nose. Quickly she wiped away the almost invisible fleck of plaster. *He must have been looking mighty hard.* The thought made her smile. *Wonder what it would take to make that one over,* Michelene thought, visualizing the man she'd just met as she waved good-bye to Marie, who was on the phone.

He'd probably clean up real good, too, even though he was an arrogant SOB. She smiled to herself and stepped onto the elevator.

Marie looked up when her boss approached. "Please hold," she said into the mouthpiece and pressed the red button.

"What can I do for you, Mr. Alexander?" she asked with a

smile. Chase Alexander was her favorite of the three partners, although he was also the most serious. But she was really happy that he'd decided to stay with the firm and not take the offer in New York that came shortly after his arrival. Although the prestige may not be the same in Louisiana as in a leading post with a big-time New York law firm, the threesome brought a degree of class to the practice of law that couldn't be topped in her book, and Chase's expertise in criminal law made the trio a formidable force.

Chase leaned down, bracing his palms flat on Marie's desk. "I need you to make an appointment for me." He pulled the gold and black card from his shirt pocket and handed it to Marie, whose brows rose in question. "Tell Ms. Tyner whenever it's convenient for her, I'll make myself available."

Chapter Two

Surprise! Surprise!

"I'll meet you at The Place about six o'clock?" Michelene said, speaking into her cell phone as she cruised down Charles Street.

"Sounds fine." Lisa held the phone between her shoulder and her ear while boxing a marble abstract statuette, which had just come in. Her facial expression contracted as if she'd bit down on a lemon. "People have the strangest taste," she mumbled, sealing up the box.

"Huh?"

"Nothing. Sorry you couldn't stay longer today. We could have gotten together for a hot minute."

"Believe me, the way my day was going, a hot minute would have taken too much time."

"I don't know why you don't get some help, Miki. At least someone to run the errands." Lisa sighed, taping the box shut.

"What's wrong, Lisa?"

"Just tired—a lot. And I can't seem to shake this cold."

The wings of apprehension momentarily fluttered through Michelene's stomach. "Have you been to the doctor?"

"No. I'm sure it's no big deal. I just need some rest and some vitamin C." She forced a laugh, then started coughing.

"That doesn't sound like something vitamin C can cure. I still say you should go to the doctor."

"I will. I will."

"Anyway, I'll see you tonight."

"Definitely."

—❈—

Michelene slid the phone back into the charger, her tapered brows wrinkled with concern for her friend.

She knew she hadn't been spending much time with Lisa lately—with their schedules being so full, it was difficult but actually it was Lisa who'd broken their last three hang-out dates, saying only that "something had come up." Michelene knew, or at least she thought she knew, that the "something" was a man. And knowing that, or at least thinking she knew that, she couldn't understand why Lisa wouldn't tell her about him. That hurt.

She and Lisa had been friends since third grade. They'd done everything together, and were closer than most sisters, so much so that people who saw them together invariably insisted that they looked alike. They both enjoyed the same things and both had majored in fine arts. Lisa decided to go the gallery route, and Michelene took her show on the road. Yet they had remained inseparable.

It was Lisa who comforted and made the arrangements when Michelene's parents died within a month of each other. Her father from a heart attack and her mother from a broken heart.

But over the past few months, the dynamics between them had been shifting. Lisa seemed to have ebbed, intentionally wanting to stay away from Michelene to avoid talking about whatever or whomever it was that had become the undertow of their relationship.

Michelene blew out a breath as she stopped for a red light, absently tapping her fingers against the steering wheel to the beat of Grover Washington Jr's classic, Mr. Magic. Maybe Lisa was tired. It could be as simple as that. Unfortunately, her gut feeling told her it wasn't.

—❈—

By the time Michelene pulled into her driveway, it was after 3:00 P.M. On her way in, she'd stopped at her favorite bakery in the French Quarter and picked up a pound of pralines. At the market she purchased three pounds of crawfish, seasonings and fresh vegetables. Food. Her one vice. She loved to eat, and loved to cook even more.

Cooking always gave her a deep-down good feeling submerging her in memories of her mother, the moments they shared together. Her mother had considered herself a gourmet cook, enlisting Michelene to work in the kitchen from the time her head could crest the kitchen table. Lena Tyner would take Michelene's little-girl hands and help her knead dough for pies, or let Michelene sit on her lap while she peeled the shrimp for gumbo. Lena taught her daughter everything she knew, and Michelene added her own special touches. To her, cooking wasn't a chore, it was more of a celebration of her mom.

She smiled as she put her packages on the kitchen island countertop, recalling those happy times. Shrugging off her jacket and stepping out of her shoes, she washed her hands at the kitchen sink, filled a pot of water, adding her favorite spices, and put it on to boil. Then she put the crawfish into a bowl of water and lemon to soak. She knew she would have a long day tomorrow and wouldn't have time to cook, and since she was eating out tonight, she'd have one of her favorite dishes prepared when she dragged herself home the following evening.

Humming softly, she diced up mixed greens, onions, peppers, tossed it all together in a bowl then into the pot of now boiling water.

With her vegetables simmering and the crawfish soaking, Michelene made a quick stop into her office to check messages. The red number flashed six. She pressed the Play button, sat down at her desk and pulled her notepad toward her.

Percy had called wanting the handmade lingerie he'd ordered for his "friend," in two additional colors. Smiling she shook her head and made a note. Then there was a message from her insurance agent, a call from the mayor's wife gushing over the linens, a hang up, a call from Paul wanting to take her to dinner and a call from Marie.

At first she thought Marie's call was about Lance. Her eyes widened when she heard Marie tell her that Chase Alexander, the new senior partner, would like to make an appointment at her earliest convenience.

She played the message back, then slapped her palm on the desktop. "Hot damn!" This was just what she needed to expand her client base. Obviously Lance told this Mr. Alexander how pleased he was with her services.

A big, bold grin split her face. She hurried back to the kitchen and retrieved her palm-top from her purse.

Quickly she scanned her appointments for the following day. If he didn't have a problem with coming by her house, she could squeeze him in for about an hour and a half. And too bad if he did have a problem. She liked doing her initial interviews with potential clients in her home office anyway. It gave her a sense of control by working on her own turf. Besides, once she was set up with a client she was pretty much at their beck and call, trying to satisfy their every whim. Going out of their way once was a small price to pay for what she put out.

Michelene keyed in the tentative appointment then jotted down a note on a yellow Post-it to call Marie in the morning to set things up with Mr. Chase Alexander, and stuck it on the screen of her PC.

Hmm. Wonder what he looks like? she mused going back into the kitchen to stir her greens. *I just hope he isn't hard to please.* From what she did know about the company, he'd joined the firm a bit less than a year ago, and it was only in the past six months that he'd had his name added to DuBois, Merchant.

She looked up at the wall clock, then automatically checked her wristwatch. She had a little more than an hour to get ready and get to The Place by six.

Lowering the flame under the greens a notch, she put the crawfish in the pressure cooker and dashed upstairs for a quick

The Place didn't take reservations. Kenny Loure, the owner, decided when he opened his restaurant that he would provide service for everyone, as long as you got there early. So as usual, The Place was crowded. People came from all across New Orleans to get a taste of it. On any given night there would be a line waiting for tables.

The building, once renowned as a house of "ill repute"—before Kenny stepped in—with "ladies of favor" beckoning the men from their balconies, was now the hook that drew everyone from far and wide. Kenny enlisted some of the most beautiful women and men in New Orleans to prance around, pose on the balconies, cater to his guests and inform them of the night's activities, ranging from famous musicians and singers to fashion shows—the clothes provided, of course, by Michelene.

Patrons of The Place never knew what the lineup would be and that was the attraction, along with the incredible cuisine.

—⊰◈⊱—

When Michelene stepped inside the dimly lit showplace, she was greeted as always by Kenny who took up his post as soon as the doors of The Place opened for dinner.

"Miki." His warm brandy eyes grazed her face, before he leaned slightly down and kissed her cheek. Bracing her bare shoulders, he smiled. "You look incredible as always." The molasses quality of his voice poured slowly over her, until she felt covered in the thick richness of it with the desire to lick the sweetness of his words.

"*Merci*, Ken." She brushed her index finger along his smooth caramel cheek, and smiled. "So do you."

"One day, Miki, you're going to stop playing games and take me seriously," he said, his tone playfully scolding.

17

"Now, Ken, if I took you seriously, it would ruin the fun we have teasing each other." Dawn spread slowly and majestically over her face, illuminating everything in its path. "That's what makes things interesting."

"Cher, one day..." He brushed a curl from her forehead. "Lisa is at your usual table." He raised his head, jutting his smooth chin to signal for one of the hostesses. "Chantelle will take you to your table and be your server tonight."

"New?"

"Yes, but good." The corner of his mouth curved and his eyes darkened.

Michelene smiled, her finger swishing back and forth as she spoke "Naughty boy, Kenny."

"You leave me no choice, Miki."

"Everyone has choices, Kenny. What one decides to do with them is the only unknown." She turned and followed the statuesque Chantelle through the labyrinth of tables, seeing instantly why Kenny would be attracted to the Iman look-alike.

Kenneth's gaze tracked her across the room, wondering what it was about Michelene that had gotten under his skin. She had an aura—a mixture of sultry aggressiveness and cool coy. She kept him off balance, never allowing him to get close enough to know if she was coming on to him, or simply being a master at the game of flirtation. Whatever it was, he couldn't seem to shake it.

He'd wanted Michelene Tyner almost from the moment he ran into her at Lisa's art gallery when on the spur of the moment he'd stopped in to look for some pieces for his restaurant. But she'd never taken his advances seriously. Or if she did, she chose to ignore them. He'd done everything in his power to win her heart: from flowers to invitations for weekend getaways to herding new clients her way to using her services to exclusively clothe his models to charm and begging. Nothing had worked. Now, he'd even gone so far as to include Chantelle in his arsenal of assault, hoping that the thought of him with another woman would spark her attention. But the truth was, he was no more interested in Chantelle than she was in him, or than she was in any man for that matter.

Absently he greeted the next guest. Michelene remained the elusive puff of smoke. He thought he could grasp her, but when he opened his hand, poof she was gone. Maybe that was part of the mystique.

Lisa looked up as Michelene approached. "Hey, girl," she greeted, putting down her drink on the rose-colored, linen-topped table, as Michelene bent and kissed her cheek.

"Seems like forever." She took a seat opposite Lisa.

"I'm telling you. My schedule has been crazy lately." She picked up her wineglass.

"The Gallery must be doing a bang up business," Michelene stated more than asked, her right brow rising to the occasion.

Lisa tried in vain to hide herself behind the mouth of the glass. "That it is."

"And why are you talking to me like you're my English teacher or something? That it is," she mimicked. "What's going on with you, Lis? We hardly talk anymore. I call you at home and all I get is your answering machine. You keep breaking dates. You—" She shook her head and suddenly started laughing. "Do you hear me? Do I hear me? I sound like I'm your jilted man or something. I know I didn't go there."

Lisa began to giggle. "Yes, you were there."

"I'm sorry, girl. I don't have any reason to jump all over you." She looked at Lisa for a moment, her expression softening. "I worry about you, that's all." She looked down for a moment, then back across at Lisa. "I mean, you're all I have, Lis. You're my sister, best friend, family, partner all rolled into one. And I feel we're drifting apart and I don't know why. There's something you're not telling me."

"It's—"

"What can I get you ladies this evening?" Chantelle asked,

smiling for some unseen camera.

Michelene looked up never more annoyed to see anyone in her life, even though she knew the woman was only trying to do her job.

Lisa ordered a refill of her wine spritzer, while Michelene ordered a Grand Marnier. Both requested the house special: spiced blackened catfish with saffron rice and a garden salad.

No one in New Orleans could cook catfish like The Place's chef, Jean. Rumor had it that he'd been offered sinful sums of money for the recipe, but had refused because of his loyalty to Kenneth.

When Jean had come to Louisiana five years earlier, broke and jobless, it was Kenneth who offered him a job and gave him a place to live until he got on his feet. Neither Jean nor Kenneth had ever regretted it.

"I'll be right back with your drinks," Chantelle said

Michelene watched her weave her way through the crowd and thought for a fleeting moment that Chantelle was almost too perfect. She blinked the thought away.

She focused on Lisa. "You were about to tell me something."

Lisa blew out a breath. "I've been seeing someone." She smiled shyly.

"I knew it. I knew it. Who is he and what's the big secret?"

"Miki—you know I love you to death and we've shared everything from chicken pox to panty hose. But—" she paused, knowing that what she was about to say could possibly change the direction of their long-standing friendship. "I can't tell you who it is. At least not now. Not until we've worked some things out."

Michelene leaned across the table, her eyes mere slivers. She lowered her voice to a challenging hiss. "Don't you dare tell me he's married. Just don't."

"I'm not," Lisa tossed back.

Michelene took a momentary breath of relief. "Thank God," she praised, then zeroed in on Lisa again. "So, if he's not married, why all the secrecy?"

Lisa pursed her lips, her eyes darting back and forth, then settled on Michelene's unwavering stare. "I don't want to say anymore about it, Miki. Please try to understand. For now. I know pretty soon I'll be able to tell you everything." She reached across the table and covered Michelene's hand with her own. "I'm happy, Miki. Really happy and I know everything is going to work out. Then I'll tell you everything. I promise."

Michelene stared at Lisa for a lengthy moment hoping to see something beyond Lisa's benign expression. There was definitely something very heavy that Lisa was hiding. But what began to worry her more was not so much the idea that she didn't want to talk about it, but the notion that whoever this mystery man was did not want his name connected with Lisa's. The question was why?

Michelene blew out a breath from between pouting berry lips. "I'll back off for now. I don't like it, but I will. But I'll be expecting you to hold up your end of this bizarre deal." She looked away for a moment then snapped her gaze onto Lisa's troubled face. "My advice, if it's somebody you have to keep a secret, then you don't have any business being with him."

"I wish it were that simple, Miki," Lisa muttered a notch above a whisper.

"Well, why isn't it?" Michelene demanded, getting annoyed at all the cloak and dagger.

"I'm in love with him."

"In love with him. Well, I'll be damned," Michelene thought nearly fifteen hours after Lisa's revelation. In all the years she'd know Lisa, Michelene had never heard her utter those words about anyone. Except her—but that was different. It was a sistah thing.

Whoever Mr. Mystery Man was, he must be somebody special. She shrugged.

Standing in front of her full-length bedroom mirror, she accessed her outfit for the day. She turned slightly from side to side trying to see how much could be seen. The deep V-cut of her salmon-toned, double-breasted silk jacket and matching broom stick pleated pants was one of her favorite daytime outfits. Though most women would opt for a blouse or a scarf under the provocative jacket, Michelene never did. The look was daring enough to be enticing, but still conventionally chic.

After pushing a pair of pearl studs through her lobes, she ran her fingers through her curls to give them an extra lift. Most people thought at first look that her sleek springy curls were the result of something out of a box. In actuality her mother had been part Native American with her father being of Trinidadian descent. She came by the curls naturally.

With coffee mug in hand, she went down to her office and switched on her computer, pulling the Post-it note from the screen. It was too early to call Milan to place the order for Percy. She'd take care of it later. But first she wanted to confirm whether or not Mr. Alexander would be able to meet with her today.

She listened to the phone ring as she examined the leather briefcase that she'd just had the local congressman's initials embossed on. She opened the soft leather case and smiled. The brown nylon dividers were delicately etched with the congressman's name in gold on every available space. That was one of the congressman's quirky fetishes. He wanted to see his name on everything he possessed.

"Folks," she said with a chuckle.

"DuBois, Merchant and Alexander," came the comforting drawl.

"Good morning, Marie. This is Michelene."

"Who obviously does not have an appointment that she's going to be late for," she said softly laughing, noting Michelene's lack of mentioning her last name. "And how are you this morning?"

"Fine, thanks. I'm returning your call about Mr. Alexander."

"Let me get the appointment book." She flipped open the thick, black leather book where the appointments and personal schedules of all the partners were meticulously kept. "Okay, when did you have in mind?'

"This afternoon at three. Here at my place of business, if that's convenient."

Marie's brows rose. "Today? I didn't think you'd be able to see him so quickly."

"I know it's short notice. But looking at my schedule for the rest of May, I'm booked solid. I wouldn't be able to schedule him until the middle of June at the earliest. If he doesn't mind waiting—"

"Hold on a moment."

With her legs crossed at the knees, Michelene rocked her right leg while she waited, taking a sip of her now lukewarm coffee. She made a face.

"Michelene," Marie said, coming back on the line. "He said three o'clock is fine. Let me get your address."

—⊸⧫⊷—

Michelene spent most of her day driving Ms. Daisy's niece, Chloe, all over town looking for fabric for her prom gown, which of course, was needed in three weeks. Meanwhile, Michelene still had to have "on the wrong side of plump" Chloe fitted.

Michelene had a blinding headache by the time they'd finally settled on a fabric that they both loved and was within the substantial budget allotted by Daisy.

She literally shouted "Amen" when she stepped across the threshold of her house. By rote she went directly into her office and checked messages, depositing her briefcase next to the desk. Depressing the Play button, she listened to her three messages, all confirmations for the following day.

She checked her watch and reconfirmed the time with the digital clock on the bookcase. She barely had a half hour to get herself together before Chase Alexander arrived.

Dashing into the kitchen, she pulled open the refrigerator door and took out the pressure cooker with the crawfish and the pot of mixed greens. Putting both on the stove on a low flame, she darted up the stairs and headed straight for the shower.

As she stood under the water for barely five minutes soaping, and cussing, she wanted to kick herself for allowing Chloe to run over her appointment time. Now she had to rush.

Turning off the water, she pushed back the stall door and grabbed the pink and white striped towel from the rod. She really had no one to blame but herself, she admitted, briskly rubbing her body dry. Somehow she was going to have to rein in her penchant for allowing people to drain her of her time even when she knew she had other things to do.

The hairs on the back of her neck stood straight up at the soft tinkle of the downstairs doorbell. "Damn"

She snatched down her peach-colored terry-cloth robe from the brass hook behind the bathroom door, cinched the belt around her waist and jogged toward the stairs. For a split second she thought about running into her room and quickly throwing something on. She didn't have time. Besides he was early.

Had she been in the shower that long? Ugh. What an impression she was going to make. Maybe it wasn't him at all but that darn Percy paying another surprise visit. She reached the bottom of the stairs, stopped, took a breath and fluffed her curls. Walking toward the door with the same confident stride as if she were on a fashion runway in a Versace original, she opened the door with a camera-ready smile.

Chase Alexander looked down into her startled gaze, the flicker of a smile tugging his mouth. The thick curve of his right brow rose in question. Mirth underscored his voice.

"Chase Alexander," he said by way of introduction. His eyes ran up and down her slender body. "Another fashion statement?"

Chapter Three

This Isn't Funny

Shoot me now, Michelene thought as she stood in her birth-day suit gift wrapped in a bathrobe, fighting to keep her jaw from dropping open. *Just shoot me and get the humiliation over with.* This was the senior partner! The man she'd thought was no more than the head carpenter. If he'd stirred something inside her then, he had no idea what he was doing to her now. He did clean up nicely.

"I hope you were expecting me," he said, boring a hole through her wall of disbelief.

She blinked. "Of course." She pulled her robe a bit tighter across her chest. "Please come in. As you can see I...was try-ing on this...robe I'd ordered...for a client—and you are early," she ad-libbed. She stepped aside to let him pass.

"Of course." He walked by her and for a split second she shut her eyes when his arm innocently brushed across her breasts. A shiver rushed through her even as she wondered how many times she'd be humiliated in front of this man, and how in the world would she be able to work with him if he made her feel like a bowl of Jell-O.

"You can have a seat in the office," she said calmly, as if she always greeted her clients in a robe and not much else. She walked around him, careful to give herself enough clearance space, and led him into the front room toward her office.

The slow, almost imperceptible sway of her hips was hyp-notic, Chase thought as he followed her, passing the kitchen and the tantalizing aromas of food that subtly wafted out, beckoning him—*"come here, come here."*

She opened the door to the office. "If you'll just have a seat, I'll be right with you."

Chase slid his hands into his pants pockets and turned toward her, an amused expression on his face. "Take your time. I have all afternoon."

Her mouth flickered around the edges in the semblance of a smile.

With as much composure as she could summon, Michelene casually made her exit and strolled nonchalantly up the stairs. She nearly collapsed when she stepped inside her bedroom and shut the door.

She pressed her back against the door and shut her eyes. "I just don't believe it," she muttered. While pulling off her robe, she marched over to the closet and snatched her sleeveless oyster-colored jersey knit dress off the padded hanger. The fit of the dress was so close, Michelene never wore anything underneath. She hated to see lines. But for the benefit of her guest, she slipped on a floral printed chiffon over-jacket that met the hem of the above-the-knee dress.

Stepping into a pair of mules that matched her dress and gave her two more inches of height, she was almost ready to face Chase Alexander.

She peered at her reflection in the vanity mirror, put on a slash of her berry lipstick, picked her curls with her fingers and added a dab of *Reality* perfume behind her ears and on her wrists. Satisfied, she rushed toward the door and was just about to run out when she realized she'd forgotten a key ingredient. She grabbed the tube of Lady Speed Stick—the unscented kind—from the vanity table and rubbed generously under both arms.

Downstairs, Chase casually meandered around the cozy office, letting the atmosphere tell him about its owner, much as a detective does at the scene of the crime. By all accounts, she possessed an eye for detail and form based on the precision and fluidity of her office and sitting room combo. Everything blended perfectly together. And she was obviously comfortable with electronics from the looks of her workspace.

The books in the four-foot bookcase covered everything from fashion to cars to house and garden to murder mysteries and romance paperbacks to computers.

His eyebrows arched briefly. Michelene Tyner was beautiful, obviously had a head on her shoulders to be able to run a successful business, seemingly well traveled and educated according to the degrees on her wall. Everything he'd heard about her was nothing less than pure adoration. Oh yes, he'd done some checking in the past twenty-four hours—from the mayor's wife to Beau, the local law officer.

She seemed to have the uncanny knack of winning anyone over who came in contact with her.

Yet in the two meetings he'd had with her so far, he'd seen a side that was both endearing and amusing. The very together Michelene Tyner wasn't always "very together." To him, that made her real, not this work of total perfection.

"I don't know where my manners are, Mr. Alexander," Michelene cooed from the doorway.

Chase turned and felt his stomach seesaw when he settled his gaze on her standing there, looking as priceless as a Rembrandt. He was wrong. She was perfect.

"What can I get you to drink? Something cool or something strong?"

Her smile was a heatwave pulsing across the room and Chase had the strongest notion to loosen his collar. She played with her words, he realized, feeling himself being drawn in. She dragged them out, tantalizing him like the aroma of good food, until the need to get closer, to hear what she had to say—savor it—was overpowering.

He blinked and slightly shook his head, snapping himself back to reality. "Something cool sounds fine."

"Lemonade? Iced tea?"

"Iced tea."

"I'll be right back." She turned away, her floral over-jacket fanning out around her.

When she left, Chase had the distinct impression that all the vitality had just been sucked out of the room with her.

—⊰⟡⊱—

Michelene was shaking all over. It took all of her concentration to keep from sloshing the iced tea across the countertop. What she needed was a stiff drink because close and personal, Mr. Alexander hit her like a live wire.

Vigorously, she shook her head and took several long, deep breaths. She had to pull herself together. Quick. There was no way that she could conduct a proper interview with her nerves and hormones on turbo.

Taking the glass, a napkin and a dose of determination, she walked back into the lion' den.

"Hope I didn't take too long." She crossed the room and handed him the glass wrapped in the napkin, just like her mama taught her.

"Not at all. Thank you." He took a sip, watching her cool, collected expression over the rim of the glass, wondering if she had any clue as to what she was doing to him with her beneath-the-lashes looks.

"Please have a seat," she said, "and I'll explain to you what I do and then you can tell me how I can help make your life easier." She gave him a slow smile.

Chase took a seat on the couch, leaned back and crossed his right ankle over his left knee and waited.

Michelene sat opposite him on the recliner, though she chose not to recline. She leaned forward, her focus totally on Chase. He felt as if she believed he was the most important person in the world.

"I started my business about five years ago with the intention of only doing clothing purchases for clients for special occasions: banquets, proms, weddings and things like that. I quickly realized that people were willing to pay for the convenience of having someone who understood their likes and dislikes—do things for them. Slowly I began to incorporate artwork, cars, linens, furnishings, jewelry, business and recreational clothing, food and...intimate apparel.

"My goal is to know my clients and their lifestyles so well that even if they call on a whim, which most of them do," she smiled, "and tell me they have a dinner party in two hours that needs to be decorated and catered and they have 'absolutely nothing to wear,' I pull it all together. I make it my business to know as much about as much as I can." She grinned.

Chase uncrossed his legs and braced his arms on his thighs. "How do you get to know your clients so...intimately, Ms. Tyner?"

Did his voice just drop a note on purpose? She swallowed as a hot flush swept through her. "Please call me, Miki."

"Chase," he volleyed.

She arched a brow. "First I start with a basic interview, which is really a getting to know you session, to see if we click. That generally takes about an hour to an hour and a half."

"And then?"

"Then we talk about my fees and—"

"Fees are not a problem." His eyes caught and trapped hers for a beat. "And you were saying."

She swallowed, rocked by the throb of his voice and the one echoing between her thighs. "And uh, your expectations. But I only anticipate covering the initial interview today."

"Is there any reason why we can't get everything out of the way today?" He shot his cuffs and checked his Rolex, then looked at Michelene. "The rest of my day is free. But if you have other things to do, I'll understand."

"I did want to try to end my day early. It's been a long week."

"No problem—"

"But...if it should take a bit longer it'll be fine." She shrugged slightly. "We could probably tie up a good deal over dinner." She caught his arched look.

"Here," she quickly added. "I've already cooked and you're welcome to join me—if we should run over time."

There, she'd put her foot in it. What was she thinking about? She cleared her throat. "At some point I visit where my clients live and work and the places they frequent. I see the type of car they drive. We visit art galleries, fabric and antique shops. But that's down the road."

"That all sounds fine to me. The idea of dinner as well."

She blew out a breath. "Well, now that we have that cleared up, I'd like to get started." She pushed herself up from her seat and walked over to her office space, opened the file drawer and pulled out a folder and several forms, then returned to the seating area.

"If you would fill these out, I'll tell you about my fees— even though you said it didn't matter," she quickly added.

He gave her an indulgent smile.

"I charge one hundred and fifty dollars per hour beginning with the first visit following the initial interview."

"As I said, it's not a problem," Chase cut in.

Michelene folded her hands on her lap. "I'm sure. But I would be remiss if I didn't take care of my end up front."

Chase leaned back, draping his arm along the length of the couch. "What you could explain to me is how you work out your billing hours." Actually he didn't care one way or the other. He just liked hearing the sound of her voice which bordered on slow and sultry, to slower and sultrier.

"There is a standard three-hour minimum for every job. More than that is billed in half-hour increments. I generally don't charge for travel time unless the client requests I come to them. I keep a daily computer record of the time spent on a project. I supply the information to the client at the end of every month along with their bill."

"What if they disagree?"

Michelene laughed. "I'm sure it's a possibility, but so far it hasn't happened. I'm very up-front with everyone about how long I think a job will take. There are no real surprises."

Chase slowly nodded, taking her in from a different perspective. Yes, she was pretty, had personality to spare and a quick wit, but she was definitely a businesswoman with a solid head on her shoulders. A lethal combination. He liked that.

"So—why don't you tell me a little about yourself," Michelene said after a long breath. Maybe if he started talking, she could get herself together and not feel like a babbling idiot when he looked at her with those piercing eyes and questioned her about basic things, which she'd suddenly felt incompetent to discuss. That's probably how he got juries to crumble to his will, she thought in a haze of tumbling thoughts and hormones. She gave him a short smile and sat back, hoping she'd be able to concentrate on what he was saying.

This was a twist, he mused, collecting his thoughts. Generally, he was the one asking the questions, compelling people to fill in the blanks, spill their guts. And he was damned good at it. He wasn't quite sure how to behave when the tables were turned. Ms. Tyner certainly didn't seem like the type who would take less than the absolute in anything. He cleared his throat.

"What exactly would you like to know?"

"Why don't you begin with the things that interest you: music, art, hobbies, cars?"

He thought for a moment. "I collect jazz albums for one, love to go to jazz concerts. I can't honestly say I know too much about art, just that I know what I like when I see it. I enjoy the outdoors. When I get a chance," he added with a grin. "Most of my time, unfortunately, is spent behind the desk or in the courtroom."

Michelene found herself once again mesmerized by his voice, but forced herself to stay focused. This was a job. Just a job. With some more gentle coaxing on her part, Chase began to open up, regaling her with stories of his childhood, bizarre happenings in the courtroom and some of the places he'd traveled.

"What made you decide to settle in Louisiana?" she asked.

Chase leaned back. "I came here about five years ago, just for a vacation and fell in love with the place, the mystique of it all." He shrugged. "I decided to take the bar exam—just in case. I met Lance at a charity function and he mentioned that they were looking for a partner with criminal experience. I thought about it, but I still went back to New York. But when my buddy Anthony Dunham moved down here—"

"The district attorney, Anthony Dunham?"

He grinned. "Yes. Why?"

She swallowed, thinking about her brief but sizzling tryst with Tony. "You travel in high circles."

"I could say the same thing about you. Mayors, politicians, the upper crust of New Orleans."

She looked at him from beneath her lashes. "You've been doing your homework."

"Absolutely. I never walk into any situation unprepared. " He stared into her eyes. "It could be costly."

There was that fluttering feeling again. She straightened in her seat, and nervously checked her watch. "So how do you feel my services will help you?"

Chase blew out a breath. "To be quite frank, Ms. Tyner, my life is in chaos. I work grueling hours, travel a lot and my apartment looks as if I just moved in a month ago, instead of more than a year ago. My wardrobe could use a good overhaul and I want the opportunity to spend some of this money I'm making on something worthwhile, something that will have some value, charities, scholarships, things like that. And from everything I'm hearing about you, you're the one who can make that happen. You have your finger on the pulse of this town, know all the right people, places and things. I want to tap into that."

"I hope I won't disappoint you, Mr. Alexander."

"I can't imagine how that would be possible."

She swallowed, then suddenly pushed herself up from her seat. "Well, our consultation time was over about an hour ago." She smiled. "I'll put this information together and get back to you. We can set up a time to meet. I'd like to spend a day with you, see your apartment, get a feel for your lifestyle."

Chase rose. "I'm looking forward to that. When should I expect to hear from you?"

"In a day or two."

"Fine." He picked up his jacket from the back of the couch where he'd left it.

Michelene led the way out, stopped then turned. "It is getting kind of late...past the dinner hour. Like I said earlier, if you'd like to stay...for dinner, it wouldn't be a problem."

His smile was slow and easy. "I'd like that a lot. If it's not too much trouble."

"Not at all. Follow me."

When Michelene closed the door behind Chase Alexander nearly two hours later, she knew she was in deep trouble.

Chapter Four

Just Feels So Right

Before Chase had left Michelene's house for the evening, they'd agreed to get together the following afternoon.

"Dinner was incredible," Chase said standing in the door-way. "Thank you. If you treat all of your clients like this, you'll never have to worry about business."

"I don't treat all of my clients this way," she responded, her dulcet tones stroking him like an expert masseuse.

"A selected few?"

Her smile was coy. "Very."

For a split moment, he had the distinct impression that she was totally coming on to him. Then in the next instant, the heat that fanned between them cooled and she had the most innocent look on her face. Maybe it was all his imagination. There was something about Michelene, a raw provocativeness coated with youthful naiveté that was an absolutely devastating combination. He was completely off balance. And he had a strong suspicion that she liked things that way. He went home captivated and totally mesmerized.

As Michelene lay staring up at the ceiling, she couldn't get Chase Alexander out of her thoughts.

What was on my mind? she kept asking herself, as the

soothing riffs of Oleta Adams crooned in the background. He must think I have a screw loose or something—the way I was practically in his lap. How embarrassing.

Her uncharacteristic behavior unnerved her. If nothing else, Michelene Tyner could always be counted on for her professionalism. Sure she used her charms along with a wink. But she'd made it a practice never to cross that fine line.

She'd been burned once with Anthony Dunham and that was enough. It had nearly ruined her. Ooh, the stories she could tell about Mr. District Attorney. The fact that he was a friend of Chase's only further complicated matters.

She turned onto her side, bringing her knees to her chest, as Oleta belted out the final chords of *Get There*. She reached toward the night table and turned off the light, cloaking the room in semidarkness. Iridescent light from the quarter moon, mixed with a canopy of stars flowed like water through the open window. A near imperceptible breeze brushed the sheer cream-colored curtains. The illuminated dial on the bedside clock showed 2:10 A.M. in bright red.

She closed her eyes and the image of Chase in her doorway, then sitting cross-legged in her office, at her dinner table, all crowded for attention behind her closed lids.

Sighing, she curled her body a bit tighter. It was going to be a very long night.

—◆—

Chase wasn't doing much better. He'd opted for prowling around his near-empty apartment, the echo of his footsteps a sad reminder of the state of his life.

Funny, he hadn't paid much attention to his private life. He'd all but pushed it into the background to make room for his career. More often than not, he didn't have the time to dwell on it. Of course there'd been a few women, but none who could hold his attention. The only one that came remotely close was Sylvia Tanner and even that had fizzled out like a flat soda. That didn't stop her from calling and stopping by on a whim, however.

And he had his share of offers, from the office secretaries to the wives of some of his clients: rich, poor, tall, short. The whole menu of temptation. But there'd never been anyone who could compare to Michelene Tyner.

He couldn't quite figure her out. The one thing he was certain of, he wanted to find out what made her tick in the worst way. There was something there. He was sure of it. As sure as he was when he held a jury in his hands and knew he could bend them to his will.

Yes, there was something. And he wouldn't be satisfied until he figured out what it was and conquered it.

Chase took a seat in the secondhand recliner, the one piece of furniture in the room, and took a sip of his rum and Coke. He stared out at the starlit night. Tomorrow afternoon couldn't come fast enough.

———⊰❉⊱———

"He's a friend of Anthony Dunham's?" Lisa asked, stunned.

"Yes. Can you beat that?" Michelene replied, talking into her cell phone while taking a wide right turn onto the highway from the one-lane road. "I almost choked."

"That's behind you. Anthony wasn't for you. It's as simple as that." Lisa started coughing.

Michelene frowned. "Lisa, you sound worst than you did the other day. When are you going to the doctor?"

"I went this morning, miss. Thank you."

"And?"

"And the doctor said I need some rest and gave me a prescription for a cough syrup. Nothing serious."

"Hmm. Well you sure sound like you need to take some," Michelene said skeptically. "And that's *all* the doctor said?" she asked over another coughing jag.

Lisa caught her breath, briefly shutting her eyes. "Yep."

"Okay. Just make sure you take your medicine. And

how's Mr. Mystery Man?" she asked waving at Beau who was supposed to be tucked out of sight behind some bushes to nab speeders. Michelene shook her head, smiled and stepped on the gas. The needle of the speedometer edged by seventy.

"He's fine," Lisa said.

"When am I going to meet him?

Lisa hesitated, fidgeted with the appointment calendar on her desk before she answered. "Soon. We'll work something out. I promise."

"Hey, who knows, maybe it could be a foursome," Michelene said on a short note of laughter.

"You're thinking about finally giving one of your many suitors some time?"

"Maybe. Kenny's really sweet, but so are Martin and Paul—well, he's a handsome thing. But—" her voice trailed off. "They don't exactly excite me. You know."

"But Chase Alexander does."

"Yeah. Too much. That's the problem."

"Well, girl, this may be one of those times when you'll have to break the house rules."

"That's a distinct possibility. Hey, I'd better get off the line or I'll be spending all of my profits on my phone bill."

"Talk to you soon, then."

"'Bye. And take care of yourself." Michelene depressed the Off button and returned the phone to its cradle. She peeked at the digital clock on the dashboard. She had two more hours before meeting Chase.

He'd wanted to meet at his office, then go over to his apartment. Her stomach fluttered at the thought.

This had the potential to turn into something worthwhile, Michelene mused. But, hey, she was getting ahead of herself. What did she really know about him? Yes, he definitely gave off signals of interest. But, so what. He could have a wife stashed away somewhere. He could have someone in his life. And then again, maybe she was just imaging his interest because hers was in high gear.

She popped a CD into the player and eased into the sounds

of Lauryn Hill of Fugees fame.

By the time she'd reached the center of town, a light mist had begun to fall. "Damn," she sputtered, alighting from the car and making a dash for the post office. She was expecting a package from Italy—a hand-painted scarf she'd ordered for Percy. Whoever was the recipient of this expensive gift was a lucky woman.

It was curious, but as much as Percy talked about his life, his rise to athletic fame and requested extravagant purchases at a whim, he never mentioned the woman or women in his life. And as much as she wanted to know, she admired him for that. A man who kissed and told was never high in her book.

After picking up her package and chatting for a minute with Glen, the head clerk, a familiar face since she was a girl, she headed for her appointment with Paul to see what kind of deal she could swing for Beau's wife, Cissy.

—⊰⊱—

"What is she looking for exactly?" Paul asked as they browsed through his catalog.

"She doesn't know what she's looking for. So I'm looking for her. I'm thinking something classy, but not too ostentatious, and plenty of room," she added, flipping through the pages.

"I could probably give you a good deal on a Benz station wagon. High quality, dependable, looks good and has space for the kids." He eased closer, standing behind her.

Michelene felt the hair on the back of her neck begin to tingle. "Sounds like a possibility," she said, ignoring the hand that was suddenly on her shoulder.

She placed her hand on top of his and gently removed it. She turned in the chair and smiled up at him.

"How about if we concentrate on what I came here for, dahlin'?"

Paul's gaze ran over Michelene's face. "Concentration is a difficult thing when you're around, Miki."

"Well, now, cher, we're just gonna have to try harder." She turned back to the pages in front of her.

"When are we going to get beyond this, Michelene?"

"Beyond what?" she asked, feigning innocence.

"This charade of acting like we don't have feelings for each other."

"Paul," she sighed, "you know I care about you. You're like family to me."

He stepped around and sat next to her. He clasped her chin, turning her to face him. "I want to be more than your friend, Miki, more than your family. You know that."

He looked so sincere, almost forlorn, Michelene thought. A part of her softened. That corner of her personality that was eager to give, to satisfy, wanted to provide for him what he wanted. But she knew she couldn't.

She let out a breath and closed the book. "Paul, we've known each other for years. Since college. We've always been friends. You help me, I help you, and vice versa. But that's all we can be. Friends. I'm not looking for a relationship."

"We could be more than friends if you give us a chance. I know it," he said, a tone of urgency edging his voice. "I could make you happy, Miki. Just open yourself up to me. Let the games go, the coyness go."

He leaned forward and before she knew what happened, he kissed her.

It was so sudden, so out of the blue, that for a moment she didn't react. But when the reality hit, she realized that all she felt was surprise mixed with disappointment. There were no shivers of delight, no rockets going off. Nothing.

When he realized she had not returned his kiss, he eased away. The look in her eyes told him everything he didn't want to hear.

"It can't happen, Paul. You know that."

Slowly he stood. "Why, Michelene? Tell me why. Tell me you don't have feelings for me."

"I do have feelings for you. You know that, but not the

kind of feelings relationships, other than friendship, are built on."

"We can work at it."

"No. We can't."

"Miki—"

"No." She smiled gently and stroked his cheek. "Friends."

Paul briefly lowered his head, then looked down at her. He shrugged his right shoulder, trying to shake off the hurt he felt. For as long as he could remember he'd been "in something" with Michelene Tyner. In-fatuated, in-awe, in-spired, in-love. Maybe he was being a fool trying to hang on when what he wanted to hang on to couldn't be held.

Michelene was as elusive as the mist that blanketed the city. The man who finally captured her would be a very lucky man.

"Maybe one of the new Jeeps would interest Cissy," he said, an expression of acceptance in his eyes.

Michelene gave him a soft smile of thanks. "Maybe it would, cher. Show me what you have."

—❖—

By the time they'd finished, settled on an Explorer and firmed up a price both Beau and Cissy could live with, it was time for her meeting with Chase.

"I don't want anything I've said to come between us, Miki," Paul said while walking her to her car.

"Nothing could come between our friendship."

He bent and kissed her cheek. "Pleasure doing business with ya, sugah."

She ducked into her car and slid behind the wheel. "Always, dahlin'." She blew him a kiss and threw a quick wink. "I'll get back to you about the Explorer."

"Tell them it's a steal," he called after her as she pulled off.

She waved from the window and was gone.

—❖—

On the ride through town, Michelene thought about the awkward interlude with Paul. He was sweet, handsome, hardworking and though she wouldn't readily admit it, she knew he cared for her deeply.

Had she led him on all these years? Had she given him reason to believe that there could be more between them than friendship? She didn't think so. She treated all men the same. Truth was, she loved men. They fascinated her. And yes, she knew she was the consummate flirt. But it was all harmless. It was one of her trademarks. And she'd gotten it honest—right from her mama.

Lena Tyner could turn a man's head and wring his heart with every breath she took. She could smile, cajole and sweet-talk a man into damn near anything. It was a work of art and a marvel to watch. And Michelene had improved on it until it gleamed like a highly polished diamond.

She sighed, turning onto Grove Street. Part of what had made her business so successful was her innate ability to get people to open up to her, trust her, feel that she cared about them and that their secrets were safe with her.

Most of her clients were whites—wealthy whites who were in a class by themselves, living in a world with views totally in contrast to reality. As a result, it was accepted and expected that she provide for them, cater to their whims. The trusted "big-house confidante." Funny, as sad as that fact was, it was the key to the success of Exclusively Yours. Her business perfected the art of catering. And as long as she could get what she wanted and not sell out in the process, she would continue to be the best at what she did. And the truth was, for the most part, she liked her quirky clients. Lord knows they couldn't help who they were.

She smiled ruefully. Those acquaintances, those secret trusts allowed her access to some of the darkest secrets in New Orleans. Quiet as it was kept, Michelene Tyner was one of the most powerful women in the city, and certainly the most powerful black woman. Maybe she couldn't change laws or increase employment, but a whispered word from her in the right ear could alter lives. And she liked it like that. Very much.

The office buildings of DuBois, Merchant and Alexander loomed ahead. Her pulse suddenly beat a bit faster. Chase.

She checked the dashboard clock then compared it to her watch. Her dark eyes widened in delight. She was actually fifteen minutes early. Maybe it was a sign, she thought. Now for a parking space.

—✵✵✵✵—

"Buzz me as soon as Ms. Tyner arrives, Marie," Chase said into the intercom.

"Certainly, Mr. Alexander." Marie clicked off and smiled, hoping he wasn't holding his breath. Michelene was notorious for being late. It was almost expected.

She turned back to her computer, slipped on her Dictaphone headset and rapidly began typing the notes being spoken into her ears. Then her fingers stopped in mid-stroke when she looked up moments later to see Michelene standing proudly in front of her.

"Hey, Marie."

Marie blinked, then glanced at her desk clock. "Michelene—"

"I have a three o'clock with Mr. Alexander."

"I know. It's not quite three yet," she said in amazement.

Michelene grinned. "Don't look so stunned, Marie. I'm trying to turn over a new leaf, get my program together. Can't always keep my valued clients waiting. Is he available yet, or should I just cool my heels a minute?"

"No. No. He said to buzz him as soon as you arrived. He's waiting for you."

"Is that right?" She felt a sudden tingle. "Well now, we can't have one of the partners wait too long. Is Lance in today? I wanted to say hi."

"Yes, he is. You can go on back and I'll buzz Mr. Alexander. His office is across the hall from Mr. DuBois'."

"Thanks, Marie."

She sauntered off down the plush, carpeted corridor, which led to the suite of offices for the partners and the associates. Lance's office was the first one on the right. She stole a glance across the hall and saw the gold-embossed name plate on the door. *Chase D. Alexander, Senior Partner.*

Hmm. Wonder what the D stands for? she mused, lightly tapping on Lance's door. *I'm sure I'll find out.*

"Come in."

Michelene inched the door open and poked her head inside. "Hi."

Lance looked up from the stacks of paper on his desk and a smile stretched like a sunbeam across his face. "Come on in here, girl," he said, waving her inside. "Standing out there like some stranger." He stood and came from around his desk.

Michelene stepped inside, crossed the Persian rug and walked into Lance's outstretched arms.

Chase stood in the partially opened doorway, viewing the scene. Something inside of him knotted and an uncomfortable array of dark thoughts tramped through his head. He knew it was innocent. Lance had no more interest in Michelene than he did in any woman. Although very few knew about Lance's personal preferences, Chase had been his friend for more than a decade. Lance, because of his profession, portrayed himself as being the ladies' man. Too bad there were still so many prejudices about gays. Lance DuBois was one of the best legal minds in the country. But let some of their international or corporate clients get wind of his "other" life, and they'd flee like cockroaches when the lights go on.

Nonetheless, Chase still didn't like the thought of a man, any man, snuggled up so close to Michelene. He knew his feelings were irrational and obviously premature, but they'd somehow burrowed their way beneath the armor he'd erected and now they were rattling him.

Quickly he turned away, went back to his office and shut the door.

—❊—

"I understand you've taken Chase on as a client," Lance said, releasing Michelene.

"Yes. We had our first meeting and I'm doing phase two today. Thanks for the plug," she teased, poking him in his muscled side.

"Anything for you, dahlin'. You've changed my life."

Lance was a bear of a man. Six feet four inches, three-hundred pounds, down from three-thirty-five, thanks to Michelene's insistence that he change his diet and attend the gym regularly. She'd hooked him up with her nutritionist friend who placed him on a diet of vegetables, pasta and fruit. The pounds had slowly dissolved. The three nights at the gym, which included a special discount, courtesy of Michelene's connections, had kept the weight loss from turning into flab. His blood pressure was down. He had more energy, and he was looking great.

"Don't wear poor Chase out," Lance warned. "I know how hard you can be on a brother."

"It's all for their benefit, sugah," she cooed, giving him her famous wink, then ran her finger down his taut belly. "Look at you. A perfect example of my handiwork."

He laughed. "Miki, you are dangerous. If I was the least bit different, I'd snatch you up in a minute." Truth was he was months into a relationship and felt that he'd finally found his soul mate, if only his partner felt the same way.

"You're sweet."

Lance's face grew serious. "Listen, I never get in your business and you know how I marvel at the way you handle yourself and your clients. But, Chase is a born and bred New Yorker. He doesn't quite look at things the way we do down her. The carefree goings-on between the sexes is taken for granted here. A way of life."

"What are you trying to tell me?"

"Just go easy on him. You could probably wrap him around your finger without trying and he'd take it all the wrong way—think there was really something to it. Understand what I'm saying?"

She looked at him a moment. A slow smile crept across her mouth. "But what if it wasn't just southern charm? What if it's the real thing?"

Lance's left eyebrow cocked, then he threw his head back and roared with laughter. "Poor bastard, he won't even know what hit him."

"Ooh, Lance, you're awful," she giggled, swatting him on the arm. "He's a grown man and perfectly capable of handling himself. New Yorkers are tough."

"I'm sure," he said over the last of his laughter.

"Do you think I have a chance with him?" she asked under her breath. "I mean, is he seeing anyone?"

For a moment Lance pursed his lips in thought. "There was someone he'd been seeing, Sylvia Tanner. You know the one who—"

"Owns the Tanner Boutiques," she said completing his sentence, while her stomach did a nosedive. Sylvia Tanner was probably the only woman in town who had a business that Michelene was loath to patronize. Sylvia was a transplanted West Coast snob who thought more of herself than her customers. Although Sylvia had some of the most exquisite originals in her shops, Michelene would rather travel to hell and back than lay one brown penny in Sylvia's hand.

They'd known each other since the last year of high school and had become quick enemies when Sylvia's boyfriend of two years dumped her two months before the senior prom and took Michelene instead. Sylvia had been trying to outdo Michelene ever since.

The idea that Chase would even be remotely interested in Sylvia Tanner certainly colored her picture of him.

"I see," she mumbled absently, then reflexively checked her watch. "Oh shit!" Her brows shot up. "I don't believe it."

She spun away, hurrying toward the door.

"What in the world is it?" Lance asked, jolted out of his musings. He was thinking of his evening ahead with his new lover.

"I was actually early for once in my life and now I'm ten minutes late," she blew out in disgust. "I'll call you," she tossed over her shoulder.

"Don't worry. No one expects you to be on time," he chuckled.

She gave him one last nasty look and was out the door.

For once she'd wanted to make a good impression on Chase. It was bad enough that both times she'd met him had been shoe-ins for *Candid Camera* moments.

Taking a deep breath she raised her fist to knock on the door, just as it was abruptly pulled open.

She put on her best smile and lowered her hand. "You weren't planning on running out on me, now were you?" she asked in her best "I almost apologize" voice. "I know how precious your time is, and how busy you are. But I was just chatting with Lance over there, seeing to his needs and all, and time just got away from me." She knew she was babbling, but she couldn't seem to stop, not with Chase's eyes boring into her soul.

He wanted to be angry with her for keeping him waiting. He wanted to read her the riot act for snuggling up so close to another man. He wanted to kiss her.

Instead he cleared his throat. "Make yourself comfortable. I'll be right back." He brushed by her and walked down the corridor.

Michelene watched his departure with an accessing eye. Chase Alexander looked good coming and going, she concluded. But how he could have gotten himself involved with Sylvia Tanner was still gnawing at her sensibilities. She wondered if they were still seeing each other.

Turning away, Michelene entered Chase's office mildly surprised at the austere decor. Everything shouted "formal," "rigid." There was nothing that made it uniquely Chase's room, unless the idea was less is more.

Michelene frowned, biting down on her bottom lip. Was this a clear indication of his personality? When they'd met yesterday, she'd gotten a sense that there was a warm, almost endearing side to him. But this room reflected none of that. She wondered if his apartment was the same. She shuddered at the thought. If that was the case, she had her work cut out for her.

She crossed the bare wood floor to where he'd hung his law degrees and awards. He'd graduated from Columbia University and had passed the bar in New York, Washington, D.C. and Louisiana. Impressive.

Taking another look around, Michelene realized that was about it for personal touches, unless you could count the name plate on the desk.

"Hope I didn't keep you too long," Chase said, startling her with his soundless return.

Her hand fluttered to her chest. "You scared me. You shouldn't creep up on people like that. Give me a heart attack and we won't get any work done."

The corner of his mouth curved upward briefly. "Sorry. I'm just about finished and then we can leave."

"I'd redo this office," she said strolling around the room with her arms folded.

"Oh, would you," he replied flatly. "Maybe I like it just the way it is."

"You can't be serious."

"Why not? It's perfectly functional, orderly—just how I like things." His gaze held hers for a brief moment before looking away.

Michelene sauntered over to his desk and leaned her hip against the edge, folding her arms acros her chest. "Trust me when I say this, Mr. Alexander—"

"Chase."

"Chase," she conceded. "I'm good at what I do. Very good. Put yourself in my hands and I'll take care of every-thing."

"It's usually me who says that to my clients."

"Think of this as a role-reversal exercise. Just like you want to have your clients' full cooperation and faith in your abilities, I feel that same way."

"And what if I agreed?" he asked from the far side of the room. "What if I just gave you carte blanche to take over my life—what would you do?"

Her right brow rose suggestively. "That's a lot of power for one woman."

He slung his hands into his pockets, crossed back and forth in front of her as he did seconds before delivering his closing line to a jury. "Let's see what a woman like you could do with all that power." His eyes narrowed slightly, magnetically holding her in place.

The room seemed to have suddenly overheated. She heard her pulse pounding like waves against the shore in her ears.

Her mouth spread in a sultry smile. "I've never backed down from a challenge, Chase. Never."

"Neither have I." He strode across the room to the door, opened it and held it for her. "Ready?"

She picked up her purse from the desk and as she walked by him, catching the heat of him, the scent of him, she wondered if she was ready.

Chapter Five

Not Another Love Affair

When Michelene stepped across the threshold of Chase's apartment and heard her breath practically echo in the cavernous layout, she knew she had her work cut out for her.

Why would he want to live like this? she pondered, as she strolled from one near empty room to the next.

The duplex boasted two bedrooms, two full baths, a kitchen that would delight Jean, the chef, at The Place, high arching windows with stained-glass tops that prismed the light making it dance in a rainbow of colors across the bare wood floors.

The master bedroom, replete with French doors, opened onto a balcony, affording an artist's view of New Orleans. At least the master bedroom appeared lived-in. She could tell he spent most of his time there. Books were everywhere, shelved, stacked—a floor-model television, one lone lounge chair draped with discarded clothing and a king-size bed, among other little accessories made up the rest of the décor.

What kind of man was Chase Alexander—really? These rooms, his office, told her that he was totally unconcerned with external pleasure. He was a basic man, with basic tastes. But she wanted to tantalize his taste buds, open him up to new flavors, new scents.

"I guess you're trying to figure out why the place is so empty," Chase said entering the bedroom.

Michelene turned away from the curtainless bay window.

"I was."

"Sometimes I come home at night and ask myself the same thing. But the truth is, more often than not, I'm too consumed by work, or too tired to care."

"Your work is really important to you, isn't it?" She slowly sat on the banquette beneath the window and crossed her legs.

He walked farther into the room. "Being an attorney is all I've ever wanted since I was a kid. I wanted to be a black Perry Mason, or Judd for the Defense."

She laughed lightly, remembering the decades-old television programs.

"But why criminal law? Why not be a prosecutor, put the bad guys away?"

"If you look around you every day, read the newspapers, watch television, listen to the radio—who do you see and hear about in jail committing crimes? Us. Black men, and now a helluva lot of black women. And believe it or not, many of them don't belong there, or even the ones who do are sentenced to longer jail time than whites doing the same crime. Why? Lousy representation."

"You sound so adamant, almost bitter."

He looked away for a moment, remembering. "Believe me, I have reason to be."

At first she didn't think he would continue, and then he began speaking, his voice taking on a distant tone.

"When I was fifteen, my older brother was arrested on an alleged assault charge on a white woman in Brooklyn Heights. My brother, Steve, had never set foot in Brooklyn Heights. But he went to John Jay High School in Park Slope, not too far away. That was enough." He blew out a breath. "The police decided to do a roundup of kids from the high school. They brought the woman in and she picked him out." He shook his head. "After that our lives were pure hell."

As Michelene listened to the pain and barely contained anger simmering in his voice, she saw an entirely new side to Chase, the vulnerable side.

"Because we were poor, we couldn't afford our own lawyer. We got a court-appointed attorney who could have cared less about my brother, or the law for that matter. He was never prepared and most of the time didn't even remember my brother's name. Steve went to jail for eighteen months and when he got out, he was never the same. He was enraged with the world, at himself. All jail did for him was turn him into the criminal he was never supposed to be. About a year after his release, he was shot by a cop during a liquor store holdup. He died in my arms in the hospital. The last thing he said to me before he died was, 'I never did nothing to that woman, Chase. I swear.'

"About six months after Steve passed, they found the guy who'd assaulted the woman years earlier. He'd been assaulting women for years. She was brought in along with a bunch of other women and they all fingered the same guy."

"Oh, God, Chase, how horrible for you and your family."

"The city finally awarded my folks one hundred and fifty thousand dollars for my brother's false imprisonment." He shrugged slightly. "My father told me it was mine to do with as I wanted. He and my mother wouldn't touch it. Blood money they called it. I called it freedom. I used it to help me get through law school."

After listening to him, she was totally breathless, vicariously imagining how awful it must have been. And wondering if the tables were turned would she have the strength to pull through something like that.

She looked across at him, his expression was remote as if the trip back in time had momentarily trapped him there. "Do you believe all of your clients are innocent?"

"It's not up to me to believe them innocent, although it helps. I have to prove them innocent. It's my job. It's what I do."

"But what if they're guilty and you get them off?"

He took a long breath and looked directly into her eyes. "Then I've done what I was hired to do—and the prosecution failed to prove their case. This may sound cold, but it's not about guilt or innocence. It's about winning your case for your client."

She was suddenly chilled and realized in that instant that Chase would be a formidable opponent—for the right price. He had a lifelong debt to settle.

She wanted to feel disgusted by his lack of outrage at a system that pandered to the survival of the fittest, by his mercenary view of the world. Even though she now understood its origins. But if she was honest with herself, looked beneath her personal sensibilities, she'd admit that she was no different, no better than Chase. Her services went to those who could pay for them—plain and simple. And she reaped the rewards.

And with that realization came a heavy sadness. Was this what life was really about—what she'd become? What was sadder still, was she didn't know any other way to be, and she believed that Chase didn't either. She took one last look at him, seeing them both in a different and not-too-flattering light.

"What happens when there's some innocent man accused of a crime who can't afford your services—like what happened to your brother? What then?"

"I do some pro bono work, volunteer stuff in the community. Money's important, but having a voice is even more important." He looked at her for a long moment, his eyes almost sad, as if willing her to understand.

"I think I should start with the living room," she said, pushing down the disturbing feelings. "It's the first room you see...the first impression you get."

━━◈◈━━

For the next three weeks, Chase and Michelene spent all of their free time together, going through catalogs, visiting antique shops, art galleries, furniture and linen stores. Neither seemed to be willing to admit that they'd totally rearranged their lives to be able to be together, even if it was under the guise of business.

They were in Michelene's car after just having completed their last stop for the day.

"I've arranged delivery of the living and dining room furniture for next Wednesday. The shipment of linen and china will arrive on Thursday," she said keeping her eyes glued to the rain-filled roads.

"The middle of the week! I'll probably be in court. You should have told me first—I—"

"It's not a problem. I can be there to accept the shipment," she soothed, now quite accustomed to his sudden bursts of frustration. Chase was entirely too tense, she thought on many occasions, this being one of them. He needed to loosen up and enjoy himself. "I do it all the time," she added, giving him a quick sidelong glance. "That's why you pay me so well, cher." She smiled to herself when she saw his tense expression soften. "Just get me an extra set of keys and I'll let myself in."

A sudden image of a near-nude Michelene wandering around his house, like she belonged there, waiting for him to come home at the end of the day, shot through him like a jolt of electricity. He balled his hands into fists, almost as if he could fight off the rapid rush of heat that had collected in his loins.

"You know what you need, Mr. Hotshot Attorney?"

"I'm sure you'll tell me."

She pursed her lips. "You need some fun, some good food, live music and some real entertainment."

"According to you."

"Absolutely. I haven't steered you wrong yet. You have to admit that. And I know just the place." She made a quick right turn, spewing up an avalanche of water in her wake.

"Where are we going? I have work to do."

She ignored him and just grinned.

"Michelene!"

"Relax, sugah. It's on me. I'm gonna spend some of that fat check you made out in my name. And I'll have you back in plenty of time to be tucked in for the night."

Chase stared at her profile and couldn't help but smile. As

much as he may protest being dragged from one end of New Orleans to the other, looking through more catalogs than he'd ever seen in his lifetime, and in and out of every kind of shop imaginable—he loved it. He loved every minute of it.

Michelene provided the spark in his life, the light that had been missing for so long. At times, he felt as if he were being propelled along the wildest ride of his life with Michelene as the conductor.

He found joy in her laughter, the mischievous twinkle in her eyes. He marveled at her business skills, her eye for the tiniest detail and her precision with every item, price, color, size. But what was most amazing and kept him in a state of incredulity was her effortless ability to get whatever she wanted, when she wanted it and how she wanted it. People adored her and were always willing to go out of their way to see that she was happy. It was her ability to make everyone she met feel singularly important. Men fell totally under her spell, but it was all good-natured.

And with every day he spent with her, he found he wanted to spend more. Was he falling for her, or was he just another hopeless soul who'd been snared under her magical spell? Him and Michelene. The idea intrigued him. But what would it take to capture her attention and keep it? Could anyone? Could he?

"Would you mind telling me where I'm being hijacked to this time?" he asked, trying to sound put out in an attempt to shake off the sudden rush of warm feelings for her.

"Ever been to The Place?"

He frowned slightly, trying to recall what he'd heard about The Place. "No."

"Good. It'll be an experience."

"You're determined to take over my life," he grumbled.

"No. Just give it a little spark, that's all."

He checked the clock on the dashboard. "If I remember correctly The Place is pretty hard to get into this time of the evening."

Michelene laughed. "Not a problem. The owner is a friend

of mine."

Chase leaned back in the seat and shook his head. "I should have known. Is there anyone in this town that isn't a close, personal friend of yours?"

She thought about it for a minute. Maybe this was her opening to bring up Sylvia. She'd avoided the issue for the past few weeks since she'd gotten the scoop from Lance. But she was never one to miss an opportunity.

"Actually, yes," she hedged, gauging his level of interest from the corner of her eye.

"I don't believe it. They must be deaf, dumb and blind. But I could still imagine you wheedling your way into their good graces. Who is it?"

"Sylvia Tanner."

She caught the flinch in the muscles of his face. The momentary widening then relaxing of his dark eyes. If she hadn't been really looking for a reaction, she would have missed it. Chase was pure control.

"Really." He cleared his throat. "Why is that?"

Casually she went on to tell him about the incident that had been the catalyst for their fractured relationship.

"But that was years ago," he said once she'd finished.

"It may have been, but that hasn't changed Sylvia's sour attitude, or unethical business tactics."

"Unethical?"

"Believe me, sugah, there's nothing I don't know about folks in this town. It's a wonder she's still in business." She suddenly angled her head in his direction. "Do you know her?" Her heart beat faster. Would he lie?

"As a matter of fact, I do."

"Really. Well—what do you think of her?"

"I haven't had any business dealings with her."

"Oh. What kind of dealings have you had?"

"Is this part of my dossier?"

"Not necessarily. Unless it's relevant." She turned to him and smiled.

"What would make it relevant?"

"If your...relationship with her—not that I'm saying you have a relationship—but, well, you know what I mean. Your interaction with her...if that would have some...effect on your interaction with me...with what we're doing."

Chase struggled to keep from smiling. So this was where the conversation was heading. "Are you asking me if I'm involved with Sylvia? Is that what you really want to know?"

"Of course not," she shot back, escaping to her defensive wall. "That's none of my business."

"You're right. It isn't."

His statement hung in the air between them, vibrating like a tuning fork.

Once again, he'd made her feel ridiculous, she silently fumed. How was he always able to do that?

"But," he said, breaking into the silence. "I wouldn't want the wrong idea to spring up between us. So in answer to your question—I've gone out with her several times. We met at a charity function not too long after I moved into the city." He stole a quick glance at her profile. Her expression was unreadable. "But it fizzled out after a few months."

"Oh." Did he hear the relief in her voice?

"Don't you want to know why?" he taunted.

"Only if you want to tell me."

"Sylvia was more impressed with herself than anything else, to put it simply."

"That's an understatement," she mumbled.

He smiled. "So, does that answer your question?"

She turned to him and said sweetly, "I don't recall asking one, cher. But thank you."

He looked at her and shook his head. Michelene Tyner was something else.

─=≈◆≈=─

By the time they'd found a parking space and made their way down the now foggy street to The Place, the line to get in was out of the door.

"Hey there, Michelene," Bobby, who stood guard at the door, greeted. "See you brought a guest tonight."

"Sure did, Bobby. Can you imagine he's never been here before?"

"Well you're both in for a treat tonight. Come on through."

"Bobby, this is Chase Alexander. Big-time attorney over at Lance's office."

"No kiddin'." He stuck out his hand. "Pleasure to meet you."

"You, too," Chase replied, nearly wincing under the vise-like grip of Bobby's catcher's mitt hand.

"How're Annette and the girls, Bobby?" Michelene asked as they stepped inside the semidarkened interior, and was immediately greeted by the jazz sounds of a live band.

"Everybody's just fine, thanks."

"You tell Tammy when she graduates I'm gonna have a big surprise for her."

"You spoil those girls rotten," Bobby fussed, feigning displeasure.

"They love it and I love doing it. See you later."

"Enjoy."

"Bobby has three girls," Michelene whispered to Chase. "One of them was born a little slow—Tammy. She'll be getting out of eighth grade and I promised her a collection of hand-carved African dolls. She'd seen some in a gallery I'd taken her to and fell in love with them." She smiled. "Sweet child. I was so glad when I found out about that special school for her. Ever since she's been there, she's just bloomed. Oh, I better make myself a note to order the dolls," she mumbled, digging into her purse for her palm top. She keyed in the information while they waited at the podium to be seated.

She was absolutely an incredible woman, Chase thought as he listened to Michelene and saw the warmth in her eyes when she spoke about the little girl. She was a giving woman and really cared about other people. His estimation of her moved up another notch and the warmth that had been growing day by day grew warmer.

When Michelene looked up from entering the information, Kenny was standing in front of her.

"Well, Miki." He leaned down and kissed her cheek, while clasping her shoulders. "Looking stunning as usual."

"Thank you, sugah. Kenny Loure, this is Chase Alexander. Chase, Kenny is the owner of The Place."

"Pleasure," Chase said, shaking Kenny's hand.

"The Chase Alexander from DuBois, Merchant and Alexander?" Kenny asked.

"The same."

"Hmm. I expected you to be older from all the glorious courtroom feats I've heard about you."

"Sorry to tarnish your image," Chase said, not sure if he liked this guy who obviously had his eye on Michelene.

Kenny chuckled. "No harm done." He turned to Michelene. "Lisa's not here tonight. But I'll have Chantelle get you two settled." He raised his hand to signal Chantelle, then lowered his head until his mouth was inches away from Michelene's ear. "Doesn't seem like your type, cher. Kind of stiff," he whispered.

"I would hope he would be," she said. "Stiff, that is." She saw his mouth twitch and knew she'd hit a chord even if it was at Chase's expense. She gave her patented wink and followed Chantelle to their table.

Inexplicably she'd wanted to defend Chase. She knew what she'd said alluded to the idea that something was going on between them. But she couldn't stand by and have Kenny try to diminish him in her eyes. What did Kenny know about Chase—the kind of man he was? He didn't. And it wasn't his role to speculate on who was right for her and why.

That's probably what she should have said instead of what she did, she mused as she took her seat. But she just couldn't resist the opportunity to take the wind out of Kenny's sail. He was sweet and all, but sometimes his concern for her crossed the line.

"Known him long?" Chase asked after they'd been seated.

"Who?" Michelene asked innocently.

"Kenny."

"About fifteen years."

He nodded and took a sip of water, took a quick look around at the near-capacity crowd. All but a half dozen tables were taken by every manner of man, woman, and those in-between. Champagne flowed. Waiters and waitresses hurried around the circular tables replenishing empty appetizer plates and taking dinner orders. On the far side of the restaurant, which was separated from the main dining room, what appeared to be a fashion show was taking place. A balcony wrapped around the upper level and opened to the outside. Every space on it was occupied with bodies, styling and pro-filing, as they did their thing for those outside wanting to take their place.

"Is there something you want to know, Chase?" She leaned forward, propping her chin up with her hands.

"Asked and answered."

"Sounds like lawyerese," she replied.

His eyes narrowed. "Meaning?"

"Meaning that you're hiding behind your profession to ask what you really want to know. What you want to ask, as a man—not a lawyer—is if anything is, or has been going on with Kenny and I. With me and anyone. Isn't that right, Mr. Alexander?"

"Perhaps I could accuse you of the same thing with Sylvia."

She smiled slowly. "Guilty as charged. Now ask me what you really want to know."

He tossed the question around in his head. He'd never been an evasive type of man. He was always direct, to the point. But with Michelene, it seemed as if all his circuits weren't functioning properly. She unnerved him, and he knew if he voiced what was really on his mind, it would take their "interaction" to an entirely new level. Is that what he wanted?

"What if I asked you if you're seeing anyone—what would you say?"

"I'd say no, Chase. I'm not seeing anyone." She held his

gaze a moment. "But I'd like to." Her heart began to thump in her chest. "And I'd like to see you—if you're not—"

"No, I'm not."

For a moment they simply looked at each other from across the table, knowing that they'd crossed that invisible line and each wanting to savor the moment.

"I feel the same way," he said softly. "I want to know you. The real you, not the businesswoman, just the woman."

"How about if we started that process tonight, right here?"

"You've mapped out every other area of my life—why not this part too?"

"I like the sound of that. And," she reached across the table and took his hand, "You know I'm very good at what I do."

Michelene and Chase strolled through the French Quarter, along infamous Bourbon Street, after leaving The Place, taking in the cacophony of sights and sounds. Low-down blues music floated out of a club they passed, mixed with finger-popping jazz right next door. Hordes of people, in all sorts of outrageous outfits, poured in and out of the countless restaurants, eateries and bars. The scent of gumbo, crawfish, stew, bisque and jambalaya wafted through the night air tantalizing their already full bellies.

Neon lights flashed from souvenir shops with hawkers beckoning the unsuspecting tourists into the domain of the overpriced collections. On one corner, a full blues band had set up shop, rivaling the music coming from the open doorways of Preservation Hall. A light fog hung over the entire area giving it a sense of the surreal.

From the balconies of the one-time brothels, couples lingered over the edges locked in an array of erotic embraces. The one-time mansions and houses whose exteriors presented neat facades and ornate grillwork still dominated the milieu. You could almost see the steamboats of old that had once chugged up and down the mighty Mississippi River, the scent of it hovering above. Energy pulsed like a heartbeat from every cobblestone, window pane and doorway.

This was the New Orleans of Storyville, the gin mills, barrel houses, creep dives, gambling parlors and honky-tonks. It was the home of Dixieland jazz, of Buddy Bolden, King Oliver, Sidney Bechet and Louis Armstrong. Michelene was in her element. This was home, and she couldn't imagine ever living life anywhere else.

"Did you grow up in New York?" she asked as they stopped in front of a bakery, inhaling the intoxicating aromas.

"All my life."

"I've visited there a few times," she said. "But I could never live there."

"Why not?"

"I didn't feel a part of things, you know. There was no sense of community. Everyone was always racing from one place to another. Not enough trees and land. Everything was concrete. How could you stand it?"

He laughed. "You get used to it, I guess. Especially when you don't have anything to compare it with."

"I would never raise a family in New York," she said, shaking her head definitively. She stopped by a street merchant and purchased some salt-water taffy.

"Do you think about having a family?"

She turned and gazed at him. He kept his focus straight ahead. "Sometimes. If I find the right man."

They moved away from the bakery and continued down the crowded avenue, walking by a boy of about ten who was tap-dancing for coins, accompanied by a man who looked like his father, keeping the beat with the rhythmic shake of a tambourine.

Chase tossed two one dollar bills into the box on the ground, to the delight of the old man.

"What's the right man for a woman like you, Michelene?" he asked as they continued walking.

"Hmm. Someone who is sure of himself. Caring. Is willing, really willing to open his heart to me and me to him.

Someone I could laugh with and share my day with. Someone I could trust and love for the rest of my life." She looked up at him. "Have you ever been in love, Chase?"

"I thought I was."

She handed him a piece of taffy. "What happened?"

"Found out I wasn't," he said shortly, taking a bite.

She wanted to pursue the line of questioning, but she sensed that he'd shut down. "Want to listen to some music?" she asked, trying to draw him back out. "There's a great jazz club just up the street."

"She hurt me," he said suddenly.

Michelene stroked his arm. "What happened?"

"She married my best friend." He chuckled, but there was no humor. "Or who I thought was my best friend."

She lowered her head. "I'm sorry."

"Don't be. It's in the past."

"I don't think so."

He glanced at her.

"It's hard for you to trust, so you bury yourself in work. You stay clear of any relationship that would require you give anything of yourself."

"You're way off base." His expression darkened like the heavens before an impending storm.

"Am I? I don't think so. Chase, my job, my life is knowing people. Understanding what they think, what they feel, letting them know what it is they want. And what I see in you is someone who's dealing with the bare minimum. You don't care enough about anyone, or anything other than your job to make a real go of it. Look at how you live, how you dress, the way you treat me. You're afraid of feelings, your feelings."

"Oh, so because I don't fall all over you like every other man you meet, I have the problem," he ground out, his temper rising.

She stopped walking and faced him. "Show me something different, Chase. Be spontaneous for once in your life. Kiss me. Right now. I dare you to prove me wrong." She looked up into his eyes, challenging him to the duel with his conscience.

He grasped her shoulders and eased her to him. His eyes raked over her face. "Don't ever dare me, Michelene."

The revelers swarmed around them, seeming to push them closer together, as his head lowered and his mouth covered hers.

Firecrackers exploded in the background, and Michelene could have sworn it was her heart.

For the balance of their evening together, they held hands, the way new lovers do. Cautious, but clinging, almost in awe of the possibilities.

Joy bubbled through Michelene. She felt as if her whole body was one big smile and everyone she passed could see it. Every now and then she'd steal a glance up at Chase and catch the ghostlike grin that played around his delicious mouth.

They walked back to her car completely comfortable in their silence, taking these, can't-go-back-to times and memorizing them—the smells, the sights, the feelings of each.

Once inside her car, shut off from the magic of nighttime New Orleans, they were confronted with their budding reality.

"How's this going to work?" Chase asked, before she started the car.

"However we want it to. And I know I want it to work."

He angled his body toward her and cupped her cheek. "How do you know?"

"Because what I'm feeling, I want more of it. As much of it as I can get, as often as I can get it."

He tossed his head back and laughed. "Sounds like woman who knows what she wants."

"And what about you?"

He let out a breath. "It's been a long time for me, Michelene. A very long time since I've really been involved with someone. Whatever is going on between us was so sudden it hit me like a two-by-four. I don't know how much I'm willing to give, or even how much I'm willing to accept. The only thing I'm sure of is that I want to be with you. I want to hear your laughter. I want to experience that feeling I keep getting inside when I see you, or talk with you."

Her eyes danced over his face. "Hey, I think it's a great beginning. But you know what?" She leaned a bit closer. Her voice dropped a note. "I think we should really practice the kissing thing, you know, until we have it down to a fine—" her lips touched his—"art."

Chapter Six

This Is It

"I'll be in court until late this afternoon," Chase said into the phone, leaning back into his new plush leather chair. He ran his index finger across his recently grown mustache.

"So a quick lunch is out." Michelene checked her rearview mirror, flipped her signal and switched into the left lane—the fast lane. "I have a few stops to make anyway."

"I should be wrapping things up here about six."

"Then you can stop by my place and we'll have dinner, listen to some music." In the weeks that they'd been actually "seeing" each other, Michelene had quickly learned that she had to take the initiative in the relationship. Chase never gave away anything. If you didn't present the picture, he invariably didn't offer to draw one.

"So I'll see you about seven."

"Can't wait," she murmured into the cell phone, then clicked off.

Building this relationship with Chase was work. More work than she'd ever had to expend on a man. At times, he could almost be romantic, funny, vulnerable. At other times, he was as impenetrable as granite. She knew most of his resistance had to do with the experiences he'd lived through, not to mention the hit parade of criminals that he dealt with on a daily basis. That could definitely reduce one's trust quotient.

But those times when he'd let her sneak passed the sentinels around his heart, she knew she'd never felt such happiness. The electricity that popped between them was undeniable and when Chase let it flow, he was all the man she knew he could be—if he'd just keep the gates open.

She checked the dashboard clock, then her watch. Ten-thirty. She needed to swing by and have a chat with Paul. The principal from her old high school was interested in a nice, mid-sized family car. But she needed a good deal. Michelene promised her she'd do some checking. She only hoped it wouldn't be an awkward scene stemming from her last visit.

Moving along the roads on the outskirts of town, Michelene was always enchanted by the beauty of the Louisiana panorama. Old-world mansions, dating back before slavery, dotted the rolling landscape. Although the summer months were wicked times to be there because of the heat and humidity, you couldn't beat it for the glorious willows that hung in huge canopies, flowers bursting in a multitude of colors, and the grass that always seemed to shimmer like jade. But what she truly enjoyed were all the sounds of life around her. The music of the birds, the gentle rush of water that lapped behind her house, that trickled in streams sprouting up from the earth.

She almost wanted to open her window and inhale the rich scents, but knew better. The humidity was near ninety percent, with the temperature matching it nose for nose, a sure sign of rain. She smiled. A perfect night to be indoors with your man. She had plans for Chase Alexander. And indoors was just the place to carry them out.

—◆◆◆—

"Michelene" Paul rose from behind his desk, his six-three height towering above her petite form.

Michelene moved forward, as if strutting down the world's runway, the way she always did when she entered a room, the body-skimming lime-green chiffon and crepe ankle-length dress moving with her like a second skin. Quickly she took in Paul. There was no doubt about it. A blind woman could see that Paul Dupre was a gorgeous man. With a mixture of Creole and Native Indian, he had the warm, rich red undertones beneath an almost copper-colored skin. Hair that she would die for capped his head, full and rich, now showing the beginnings of gray at his temples and in his mustache, which only distinguished him all the more. Unfortunately, Paul wasn't the man she wanted.

A smile spread across her face as she approached, her arms open and outstretched. "Good to see you, sugah."

He stepped into her arms and embraced her, briefly shutting his eyes as he felt the length of her body brush gently against his, the soft chiffon of her dress feeling like a piece of heaven.

He kissed her cheek and stepped back. "As always you are a vision, Miki."

"You always say that, Paul."

"It's always true. Now that we've got the accolades out of the way, dahlin', what can I do for you today?"

She laughed, took a seat and crossed her legs, putting her purse on her lap. She opened the flap and took out her palmtop. Quickly scrolling down to Marion Hall, her former principal, she pulled up all the particulars of Marion's request.

As Paul listened to the needs, and what Marion was willing to spend, he perused his massive listing of automobiles he had at his disposal.

"I have quite a few things that would meet her requirements," he said, jotting down some information. He snapped the book close. "I'll check on the availability and confirm some prices."

"Great. Thanks as always, sweetie." She stood, thankful that the meeting had gone smoothly.

Paul came from around the desk and slid his arm around her shoulder as they walked toward the entrance.

"I just might be needing your services soon," Paul said as he opened the glass door for Michelene.

She turned and looked up at him. "Anything for you, sugah. What is it? Party? New furniture, wardrobe?"

"I'm getting married."

Her stomach dipped and she felt a tightness in her chest. An instantaneous flash of jealousy. "Married." The word clung in her throat.

"You don't have to look so stunned, Miki. You didn't think I'd wait for you forever, did you?" He brushed her cheek with the tip of his finger.

"Of course not, darling," she said trying to contain her shock and her wounded ego. "So who's the lucky lady?"

"Sylvia Tanner."

Her eyes widened and her mouth almost dropped open. It was pure willpower that kept it shut. "Sylvia?"

"She's really quite wonderful and she's makes me very happy, Miki."

She forced herself to smile. "I'm happy for you, Paul. Really I am. I just never imagined you and—"

"I know. It just happened."

Yeah, really. "So—when's the big day?"

"Spring of next year. You know Sylvia, she wants to do things in a big way."

"Hmm. I'm sure." She opened her car door. "If there's anything I can do, Paul, just let me know."

He kissed her cheek. "Thank you, Miki. We'll talk."

She slid behind the wheel of her car and started the engine. "Take care, Paul. And congratulations. Send my best to— Sylvia," she said, nearly choking on the sentiment.

"I will."

Paul's little bombshell had inexplicably put her in a bad mood, and she wasn't sure why. It wasn't as if she wanted Paul for herself. But it was always comforting and a boost to her ego to know how he felt about her. It was an odd sense of power. Now those feelings would be showered on someone else. Sylvia Tanner, no less. That's what truly had her riled. First it was Chase and his announcement, now Paul. Would Sylvia Tanner be her albatross into infinity? The last time she'd seen Paul he was all over her, and in the blink of an eye he's engaged, no less, to Sylvia Tanner. What in the world was that about? Men.

She stepped on the gas and headed home, determined to push thoughts of Paul and Sylvia out of her mind. Maybe they would be happy together. She could only hope.

However, her main concern was getting her own escalating relationship from simmer to boil. If there was one thing she'd discovered about Chase, he didn't move on anything too quickly. He was definitely not a man propelled by emotion. He had to be led, then convinced by all the evidence. And she was doing everything in her feminine powers to lay out the clues. She smiled. She liked her new role as the pursuer and not the pursuee. It made her use skills she didn't even know she had. Now, it was only a matter of time.

Chase looked up from the paperwork in front of him at the sound of knocking on his office door.

"Hey, Lance. Come on in."

Lance stepped into the room. "How's everything going with the Puryear case?"

"It's a mess, but I'm trying to work through the details. I just got the evidence envelope from Dunham's office."

Lance took a seat on the couch. "What are your feelings about it?"

"Honestly? I think I can win it. But there's something she's not telling me. I believe there was more to her relationship with Johnson than she claims."

Lance pursed his lips. "Enough for her to have killed the man?"

"No. But it was more than just business. I think she's afraid that if she tells me the whole story, I'll think she was really involved."

"Unfortunately that's the situation with most of our clients. They're so busy thinking they're protecting themselves, they tie our hands in defending them." He blew out a breath. "But, she's paying us top dollar to get her off. So get her off. Let her live with her conscience. It's not our job."

Chase nodded in agreement, but there was an uncomfortable twinge of doubt in the pit of his stomach. Something he'd never felt before. Conscience. Although he'd never admitted it to Michelene, her questioning of his values had him beginning to look at what he did in a different light. But, as Lance said, it was a job. A job that he was paid an exhorbitant amount of money to do.

"Place is finally looking lived in," Lance commented, cutting into Chase's thoughts. He stood and took a good look around. "Michelene's done wonders." The once bare walls now held a distinctive assortment of artwork including a classic piece, Garden of Music by Bob Thompson, stunning photos by Steve Martin and Gordon Parks and a brilliant piece by Grenadian artist Denzil Forrester, *Red Room*. The once pedestrian furniture had all been replaced with soft, brush-cotton loungers, a gleaming cherry-wood desk and a glass wall unit filled with wood and clay sculptures and cut crystal.

"That she has. Thanks for the recommendation." He returned his gaze to his paperwork, hoping that Lance wouldn't see the light in his eyes when Michelene's name was mentioned.

"How are you two getting along?" Lance asked, stepping closer to Chase's desk. He picked up a marble paperweight, turning it around in his hand.

"Fine. She's a very determined woman."

"That's an understatement." He paused a beat. "She's determined to get you."

Chase's gaze snapped up. Lance was smiling. "It's business," Chase countered.

"How long have we been friends, Chase?"

"Too long."

"Exactly. Michelene is perfect for you. Whether you want to admit it or not, the woman has had an effect on you. You don't even look the same. Your crusty manner is even beginning to fall away. You almost seem happy."

Chase held back a smile. "Very observant, counselor.

Anything else?"

"I think you should go for it. Michelene's a very special woman. You'd be lucky to have her in your life—round you out. There's more to life than just work, Chase."

He looked his friend in the eyes. "I'm beginning to see that," Chase confessed.

Lance nodded. "Have a good evening and keep me posted on the case." He turned to leave, then stopped. "Tell Michelene I said I think she's doing a fabulous job."

———⋇✦⋇———

After Lance left his office, Chase thought about what he'd said, the truth of what he'd said. He did feel different. He actually felt good inside. He looked forward to doing something other than work. He anticipated Michelene's calls, her smile, her laughter, the time they spent together. He was falling for Michelene. Who was he kidding? He'd already fallen for her. His stomach did a slow dance. What was he willing to do about it?

———⋇✦⋇———

Michelene returned home, loaded down with packages from the market. She planned on making a very special dinner for Chase. She didn't know about him but she was more than ready to take their relationship to a new level. Some days she couldn't think straight for thinking about him. Her dreams were filled with images of the two of them together. She'd rearranged more appointments than she'd ever done in her life just to be able to adapt to his hectic schedule.

"But enough is enough, Michelene," she scolded herself as she took the vegetables out of the bag and put them on the countertop. "I've never been one to sit back and let life happen to me. And there's no sense in starting now." She pulled out a bottle of white wine and put it in the refrigerator to chill. She set out the shrimp, mussels, clams and oysters. If there was any truth to the old wives' tale that an assortment of seafood were aphrodisiacs, then Chase was in for the seduction of his life. Looking at her arsenal she smiled.

After seasoning the food with lemon juice and fresh garnish, she put everything on the stove to simmer and headed upstairs for a quick shower. She wanted everything to be perfect tonight, from the food to the music to the feel of her skin beneath his fingertips.

Under the beat of the shower, she shut her eyes and imagined the strength of Chase's hands exploring the dips and curves of her body. Hot sudsy water slid down the valley between her breasts, along her flat belly collecting like diamonds on the dark tuft of hair between her thighs.

Softly she hummed as her hands, covered with soap, caressed her skin. Behind her lids, she saw Chase in front of her, his eyes dark with passion as he gazed at her naked body. He was perfect, all hard muscle. He moved closer to her under the pulsing water, cupping the swell of her breasts in his hands, gently kneading them until the tips peaked and hardened to his touch. Taking one into his mouth, suckling, she felt the heat between her legs shoot through her body, exploding in her head. She moaned and her eyes flew open.

She was alone.

Shaking her head, she quickly rinsed and turned off the water. "You have it bad, girl," she mumbled, wrapping a towel around her body and padding off to her bedroom.

—⊷◈⊷—

Returning downstairs to check on her food, she did a quick survey of her music collection, pulling out her favorite CDs and putting them on the changer. Anita Baker's *Been Gone Too Long* floated through the house. Satisfied, she headed to her office to review her schedule for the following day, just as the doorbell rang.

She frowned, checking her watch. It was much too early for Chase unless he got a reprieve at court and was able to get out early.

Retracing her steps, Michelene went to the front door, peeked out of the opening. Percy.

"Damn." Maybe he'd make it quick. She was definitely going to have to chat with him about his impromptu visits. She pulled the door open, pasting on her best smile.

"Percy. How are you, sugah?"

He leaned down from his six foot six inch height and kissed her cheek. "Always good when I see you. I'm off for the next two weeks. A break in training. But I'll only be in town for about two or three days."

She stepped aside to let him in. "Your shipment came."

"Great. I was hoping it would. I want to surprise her."

Michelene walked through the house to her back office. Percy followed.

"When am I going to meet her?" she asked over her shoulder.

"You keep a good secret, don't you?" he asked as they entered the office.

She turned to him. "Sure, Percy. It's the soul of my business."

"She's married."

She hoped her expression didn't give away her shock. "Oh," was all she could say.

"I know. It's wrong. And we're trying to work things out."

"Like what—her leaving her husband and running off with you? Percy, you're smarter than that."

"Yeah, that's what I keep telling myself." He lowered his blond head. "But I love her."

"It would kill your career."

"I know. That's why we're trying to keep it under wraps until the right time. Miki, my career is everything to me. I worked too damned hard to get where I am. I'm not going to risk it, believe me. We'll just have to wait it out. When she's finally free and clear and after enough time has passed after the divorce, then we'll be able to come out."

Michelene sat down heavily in the chair. "Percy, I can't

imagine how hard it must be on you—on her." She slowly shook her head. "Just be careful, Percy. I'd hate to see you get hurt by all this."

"Thanks." He took a breath. "So, let's see it."

Michelene got up and went to the closet in her office and pulled out the box she'd picked up from the post office.

Percy opened the box and his blue eyes widened in delight. "This is beautiful," he said, pulling the near-sheer hand-painted scarf from the tissue paper-filled box. "She's going to love this."

"It is beautiful, isn't it. It's a one of a kind."

"Just like its new owner," he said almost to himself. Thoughtfully he returned it to the box.

"Let me wrap it for you." She took the scarf and went to her collection of gift boxes that was stacked in the closet and rewrapped the gift. "Here you go," she said, handing it to him, complete with a gold ribbon.

"Thanks." He stood. "I better get going. I have a feeling you're expecting company," he teased, the tiny dimple in his left cheek winking at her.

She angled her head to the side. "That obvious, huh?"

"Very. He's a lucky man."

"That's exactly what I want him to think," she said, walking him to the door.

He turned to her at the entrance. "I'm sure I don't have to say this, but what I said, it's between you and I."

She reached up and touched his cheek. "Of course. Don't give it a second thought. I just hope everything works out for all the parties involved."

"So do I. Take care, Miki." He kissed her cheek again.

"Will I see you before you head back out of town?"

He shrugged slightly. "I'm not sure. I'll try."

She nodded. "Be well, Percy."

He trotted off, his long arms and legs quickly covering the short distance from her front door to his Jeep.

Slowly she closed the door behind him. Married. She always knew that athletes had a reputation for fooling around, having a bevy of women and groupies, but she'd never imagined that Percy would be one of them. He'd always been so levelheaded. All through his school years, all he'd ever talked about was being in the NBA, to the exclusion of everything else. He could have had any woman he wanted, but he was rarely if ever seen with anyone. He said getting bogged down in a relationship only distracted him from his goal. And now this. At the crest of his career, he gets involved with a married woman.

When Michelene took him on as a client two years earlier, she knew he'd come out of that shell of his youth. He was always buying gifts for one woman or another, but it was only in the past six to eight months or so, that he'd stop telling her to send the gifts directly to the lucky lady's home. Instead he'd come to pick them up personally. She knew something was up, but married.

She shook her head. There was just no telling what a person would do in the name of love.

Pushing the disturbing revelation temporarily out of her head, Michelene went back to the kitchen to check on dinner. Everything smelled heavenly. As she added a bit of red wine to the steaming mussels, the bell rang again. Her heart beat just a bit faster. Chase.

Checking her reflection in the hall mirror, she finger-fluffed her short curls, brushed invisible wrinkles from her ankle-length champagne-colored dress, then pulled open the door.

Before she could say a word, Chase took her in his arms and covered her mouth with his. Her heart raced as his hands roamed up and down her back, pressing her closer to his body. His tongue found easy entry into her mouth, dancing with her, teasing her, arousing her.

Her head felt suddenly light, and she clung to him.

"I've waited all day for that," he said deep in his throat, his mouth brushing against hers.

Who is this man? And how long is he staying? she thought. She ran her hands across his wide shoulders. "I have a practice of not keeping my clients waiting—too long," she added. "Had I only known, we could have done something about this a long time ago."

"You know I don't like to show my hand until I'm absolutely sure."

He stepped inside and shut the door behind him. Michelene took his hand, leading him into the living room.

She turned, looked up into his eyes. "And what is it that you're absolutely sure of?"

"That I want to see just how far we can take this thing between us, Miki. I want to be with you. Be a part of your life."

"Why, Chase? Tell me why." She brushed her thumb across his lips and witnessed the slight flutter run through him.

Briefly he looked away. "This...is hard for me."

"What?"

"Laying my feelings out. Exposing myself. It's nothing I'm used to."

"You've spent so much of you life being rational, only dealing with the facts. Emotions are ambiguous, Chase. Like vapors. You can sense them, almost see them, but you can't shape them, or make them be something concrete. They just are. And if you give yourself over to them, wrap yourself up in them, you have no idea of the joy it can bring to you."

"Is that how it is for you, Miki? Joy?"

"It's what I want. It's what I almost had once and I've waited a long time to find it again."

For a split second, a dark shadow of jealousy filled his stomach like something hot had slid down his throat, settled there, then spread. Of course Michelene had a life before him. But it was hard to reconcile the idea that she could have ever been another man's woman. He knew it was infantile thinking. He knew it wasn't rational. And that's when the moment subsided. What, if anything, about him and Michelene, how he felt, was rational?

"And you think we can have this joy thing you're talking about?" he asked, saving any questions about former lovers for another time.

She smiled. "Absolutely. And you know," she added, playing with the tiny white buttons of his shirt, "I haven't been wrong yet."

He cupped her face in his palm. "So if I just give myself over to you, what then?"

She touched her lips to his. "Why don't we try to find out." Her eyes held him as she methodically began unfastening the buttons of his shirt. She loosened his tie and slid it from beneath the collar of his shirt, tossing it to the floor.

Miles Davis' original *'Round Midnight* cried soulfully in the background. The wailing notes of the trumpeting legend seemed to vibrate through them, sensing it seemed the rise of passion between them in perfect pitch. But they changed the notes, made them their own with the play of fingers along spines, the gliding of bodies—one hard, one soft—against each other. Up the scale they danced, flesh becoming more exposed with each downbeat, every breath, until that bridge was reached—that point in the song that everyone knows, the hook, the familiar. But still it was different, because they took that old-time rhythm and turned it on its ear with the meeting of bare flesh, sweet sighs of passion, the joining of one entity to another, creating a masterwork of perfect harmony.

There, surrounded by soft light and enchanting sound, on the firmness of the wood floor, sheathed by the soft cotton of the rug, Michelene's soul sang when the unspoken chorus in Chase's heart entered and filled her body.

Her eyes squeezed shut when the surge of him sent shockwaves of pleasure pouring through her. She wanted to cry from the pure bliss of it, this moment of perfection—this first time of celebration that could never be duplicated.

She clung to him, needing to be nearer, closer to the beat of his heart, closer to his soul. With every rise and fall, a new height of ecstasy was reached.

Chase was all that she'd imagined and more. The gentle murmurings he whispered in her ear, the soft caresses along her tingling flesh, all ran in counterpoint to the deep, slow strokes that rocked her to the core of her being.

He felt as if he'd left his body. It was no longer under his control. But he'd slowly begun to realize that with Michelene he could easily lose all sense of balance. Being with her, a part of her, filling her body, transported him outside his realm of the familiar. She made his body smile in pure delight. He heard his joy bubble from the depths of him. It whispered along her neck, across the swell of her breasts; dipped into the hollow of her belly; brushed the dewy tangle of triangular hair; stirred the sleek muscles of her thighs, her legs; then rippled back through him expelled with each thrust of his body into hers.

The notes of the music arched, shuddering through them like electric charges.

She held him closer as her walls expanded then tightened around him, drawing him in, beckoning him deeper into the confines of heaven, pushing her over the horizon where the brilliance of light and life sang to the heavens in a sweet symphony of total surrender.

He felt it. The undertow that pulled him from deep within, weakening him, leaving him utterly powerless to resist the wave upon wave of erotic heat that raged like an inferno inside his soul.

This was joy.

———◆———

Later, as they lay tangled in each other's embrace, their meal finished, empty dishes and half-filled wineglasses surrounding them, they took their first step toward tomorrow.

"Do you always seduce your clients?" Chase teased, running his finger along the shell of her ear.

"This was one of those times when I decided—to hell with rules—mix business with pleasure."

"Does this mean that my rates go down? Do I get the lover's discount?"

Laughter rippled up from her throat. "I said mix business

78

with pleasure, not lose my mind." She kissed the tip of his nose. "But if you can do what we just did—and it's not some sort of crazy fluke to feel so damned good, I just might consider giving you a break.

"Oh, baby, you drive a hard bargain."

"Anything too easy isn't worth having."

He gazed down into her eyes. His voice dropped in pitch. "I'm beginning to believe that every day."

She nestled her head against his chest, listened to his heartbeat. "I can't wait for you to meet Lisa."

"Your friend, The Gallery owner?"

"Yes. I've been telling her about you. But every time I've wanted us all to get together, she's either been tied up, or not feeling well." She paused for a moment thinking about Lisa. "I'm worried about her."

"Why?"

"I just have a bad feeling. She's been sick a lot lately, and she swore to me she'd seen a doctor. But she doesn't sound any better. And to top that off, she's involved in a questionable relationship."

"What's that supposed to mean?"

"Actually," she hedged remembering her promise to Lisa. "I'd rather not talk about it. It's pretty personal."

"Hmm." He murmured. "You don't think she's getting better?" he asked changing from the obviously touchy relationship topic.

"I don't know. Whenever I talk with her, she sounds almost weak. And she has these coughing spells. But she swears she's fine. Nothing some Vitamin C and cough syrup won't cure." She sucked her teeth in disgust.

"Doesn't sound good."

"I know." She sighed. "But Lisa's a big girl. She can take care of herself."

"Just hang in there and be her friend."

"Believe me, nothing can ever change that. Even if she is stubborn. Lisa and I have been friends since first grade. She's more of a sister than a friend. Nothing could ever get between us."

Michelene closed her eyes while Chase gently stroked her bare arm. She could only pray that what she believed in her heart would remain true: Lisa was fine and was as happy with her new love as she was with Chase.

Chapter Seven

And Then Came the Rain

August. Blistering heat. Sudden, terrible lightning storms. And then came the rain. Louisiana was pummeled by it for five straight days. No end in sight. Steam billowed like cumulus clouds from the street, the combination of cool water hitting hot pavement caused pillows of vapor to rise—hanging over parts of the city like specters.

Michelene confined herself to conducting business from her home office, knowing that the drive in and out of town was too dangerous.

Static-filled news reports already noted that many daredevil drivers had been trapped in their cars by flash floods. Three drowning deaths were already reported in the papers. In some spots, phone lines were down, effectively cutting residents off from the rest of the world, which was the case with Lisa.

Michelene tried unsuccessfully to reach her since the start of the storm. Lisa was alone out there, near the bayou—where looming cypress and clinging moss shadowed everything in their path—even more secluded from her neighbors than Michelene. She could only hope that Mr. Mystery Man was with her.

Speaking of romance, Chase had promised to try to get by later than evening. Since that first intimate night together several weeks earlier, they'd been totally inseparable.

Each day, every conversation, every mind-blowing time of loving, touch, sound of laughter, brought them closer together.

Gradually Michelene was beginning to see the change in Chase, in his willingness to share himself with her.

One evening after making love, he'd told her about his growing up in New York and how difficult it was to stay away from the traps that were set to snare and capture anyone not sure of themselves.

"By the time I was ten years old," he'd confessed, "I'd seen two murders. More people than I care to count were strung out on drugs by the time I reached my teens. I daydreamed about getting out of the neighborhood, not being a carbon copy of so many of the young brothers that I saw every day. I guess when my brother was arrested and then gunned down, really iced it for me. I didn't want to see anymore brothers go down that road if I could help it."

"But a lot of them made those choices, Chase."

"Some of them didn't have a choice. If you live in a society where everything is measured by a price tag, your possessions, money and the color of your skin, what choice does a young black man have whose family history is welfare? What choice does he have when his opportunities in life were made null and void the instant he took his first breath, and who is told he is nothing and never will be more than nothing. And the only road out is the dark road. What choice is that?"

"Life was so different for me," she said thoughtfully. "Of course there's racism, some blatant, some subtle. But it's a little easier on black women. We aren't looked upon as threats, or persons to be feared. I guess I was able to take advantage of every opportunity." She turned to him. "But you made it out."

"Yes. I did. But look how—with the money that resulted from my brother's death. Yeah, I took advantage, too, and made it work for me. And my goal is to help as many people as I can for as long as I'm able."

She saw the subtle changes in herself, too, since Chase had entered her life. Her flirting, an almost silent need, had tempered. The desire to be admired, fawned over was no longer a driving force. Chase provided her with the nurturing that she'd inadvertently craved from other men.

At times she wondered from where that need had arisen and surprisingly it was Chase who brought clarity to her question.

They'd been talking about her mom, her love of cooking and her way with men.

"You certainly picked those two traits up honestly," Chase had joked.

"Sometimes," Michelene said wistfully, "I would watch my mother in awe, the way men would just about fall at her feet just to get her to smile. It was an amazing thing to watch. And she was so carefree about it. There was no put on, no song and dance. It was as natural to her as breathing."

"What about your dad?" Chase asked, taking a sip of wine. "I've never heard you talk about him."

She sighed. "Daddy. I suppose I don't talk about him much because I didn't really know him. He was there, but not there at the same time. I knew he loved me and Mama, but I'd be lying if I said he ever showed it. Mama was always trying to get his attention with one thing or the other. Most times he'd just smile, tell her something real vague like 'real nice, cher,' then go back to reading his paper.

"Sometimes I'd look in Mama's eyes and see the hurt there, an almost lonely vacancy and I'd feel so bad I'd want to cry because I knew just how she felt. I guess mama and I spent most of our lives trying to get Daddy to pay attention to us, smile at us, tell us how pretty and important we were."

"Maybe that's why it was so easy for your mother and then for you to seek the attention from other men, even if it was just harmless flirting. It soothed an ache."

She smiled at him a moment, listened to the logic of his words, registered the sincerity in his tone, the lack of censure.

Until that moment, she'd never actually examined the reasons why. She just accepted it as the way she was, the way her mother had been. But finally, all at once she understood. All those years she'd been searching for her daddy's attention and finding it in the men she encountered.

And with that realization came the simple knowledge that what she needed now, as a woman, was not the love of a father for his daughter, but the love of a man for his woman. She'd finally found it.

And she wanted to see her man. The past few days had been pure torture. She and Chase talked constantly by phone, but she'd grown accustomed to waking up next to him, whether it be his bed or hers. She missed him, and silently prayed that he'd be the gallant knight and find a way to traverse the murky waters and rescue his lady-in-waiting.

She curled up on the couch, listening to the rain pound against the front awning, bounce off the porch, as she absently munched on a bag of chips, vaguely paying attention to the afternoon newscast.

But the mention of Lisa's name made her jump to attention. Her heart started pounding as heat rushed through her.

"Gallery owner Lisa Renoir was found dead in her home on Clover Lane late this morning..."

"Lisa!" Her hand flew to her mouth.

Suddenly she felt dizzy, as heat surged through her body. Her stomach churned.

"Initial reports indicate that the trendy gallery owner may have been the victim of a break-in. No further details are available at this time."

Her brain completely fogged over. It was as if she couldn't make sense of what she'd heard. She started to shake violently as her thoughts began to take shape then spin in chaotic disarray.

Denial ascended to the forefront of her emotions. It had to be a mistake. But it wasn't. Something inside of her knew it wasn't. "Oh, God, not Lisa!"

She ran to the phone, tears hampering her vision. But who would she call? Who could tell her that what she'd heard wasn't true?

Before she could pick up the phone, it rang. The shock of it stopped her hand in mid-air. A chill spread through her effectively shutting down the waves of heat.

Her hand trembled as she picked up the receiver, bringing it to her ear.

"Hello?"

"Michelene. Oh, God, Michelene! My baby. My baby is dead."

The keening wail of Lisa's mother joined her own tortured sobs, their pain echoing throughout the town house out into the rain-soaked night.

—◆◆◆—

Chase rocked Michelene throughout the night, cradling her body against his, wishing he could absorb some of her hurt.

He understood her loss, the overwhelming feeling that something inside of you had died as well. It was the way he felt when he lost his brother, Steven. But unlike Michelene, he had no one with whom he could share his pain.

His parents retreated into their own world of grieving, angry silence forgetting that he'd lost Steven, too. Thank God he'd found a way to heal, or at least found a way to piece himself together enough so that he could move on. There were still some chips around the edges, some fragments that still needed mending. But overall, he was better. And Michelene would be one day as well. He'd see to it, be there for her for as long as she needed him.

"I told her about living so far away," Michelene moaned. "Out in the middle of nowhere. I told her," she sobbed. "She was my sister, Chase. The only family I had after Mama and Daddy died. What am I gonna do without her?" Her body shuddered with a new onslaught of tears.

Chase gently stroked her head. "You're going to move on, Miki. As painful, as impossible as it may sound, you must and you will. And I'm going to be here every step of the way."

"Will you?" she asked, her voice tiny, almost doubtful.

"I love you, Michelene." He kissed the top of her head, hearing the echo of his words dance in his head. Now that the words were out, his entire being felt light, free.

"Love me?" She angled her body to be able to look into his eyes, his heart.

"Yes, I love you and I'm going to do everything in my power to take your pain away, make you whole and happy again. The way you've made me. I promise you."

—※◆※—

The next few days Michelene felt as if she were in a trance. She barely got through her days. She'd canceled all of her appointments to help Mrs. Renoir make the arrangements for Lisa. As difficult as it was, the act of doing something constructive helped to keep her sane. That and the recurring chant of the words I love you that Chase had spoken on that night. It was her light at the end of that very dark tunnel. One which she couldn't wait to reach and savor once the ordeal was behind her.

There were still no leads on a suspect. All the police were certain about was that Lisa Renoir was dead. They'd refused to release details of how she was killed. The full autopsy report was still pending, and Lisa's apartment was off-limits. A crime scene, the police told Mrs. Renoir. And until some resolution could be brought to the case, no one but the police and the crime lab personnel had access.

Chase was incredibly supportive. Just when she thought she'd break, he was there to comfort her. In an odd way, Lisa's death drew them closer together. It also helped Michelene to see a soft, tender side of Chase that he rarely displayed. And for the first time in her life, she'd allowed herself to rely on someone else for a change. Instead of her determining the wants and needs of everyone else, it was Chase who anticipated her every desire and made it happen.

She'd never responded in kind to Chase's declaration of love, she realized as she slipped into her black Chanel dress. Looking at her reflection in the full-length mirror, seeing beyond the hurt in her eyes, she saw the love she possessed for Chase—felt it like a warm ball in the center of her chest. And as soon as this was behind her, she would tell him—show him and tell him some more.

The downstairs doorbell rang, sending a sharp pain to her heart. She knew it was Chase. It was time to put Lisa to rest.

It was time to go.

—⊰⧉⊱—

Michelene wasn't too sure how she'd gotten through the service. Perhaps it was seeing the throngs of people who filled the church, or the funeral procession that ran for blocks, the mourners clad in all black, tapping tambourines and speaking through trumpets that cried the blues.

She thought about that now, as she sat propped up in bed, sipping a cup of cinnamon-apple tea and watching the news.

Lisa's funeral was nearly a month ago, but the ache at times was still as strong as if it were just happening. All she could pray for was that one day at least the loss would be bearable and that the one responsible for taking Lisa away from the world would pay.

When she focused on the screen, Percy's face filled it. At first she figured it was just another announcement about his basketball heroics on the court. But what the newscaster said made her blood run cold.

Chapter Eight

All That Glitters

Michelene couldn't stop her heart from racing and her fingers shook uncontrollably as she punched in the numbers to Chase's office.

"Merchant, DuBois and Alexander," announced Marie.

"Marie, it's Michelene," she said in a rush. "I've got to speak to Chase."

"Good Lord, Michelene, what on earth is wrong?" she asked, her own tone rising a notch from the near-frantic quality of Michelene's voice. "Mr. Alexander isn't here. He's still in court. Tell me, maybe I can help you."

Everyone at the firm knew about Michelene's and Chase's relationship and Marie had become accustomed to Michelene calling for Chase. But never like this.

"Did you hear the news?" Michelene demanded more than asked.

"No. What happened? Is it about Lisa?" Marie had known Lisa well and had purchased several pieces of art from her over the years. She was as baffled and hurt as anyone over her death.

"Yes. They said they're holding Percy Hawkins as a suspect."

"What?"

"He killed Lisa!" she screamed into the phone, the horror of it, the realization suddenly erupting with volcanic force.

Marie made a quick sign of the cross. "Miki, please, calm down, honey. We don't know anything for sure. Maybe—"

"Don't patronize me, Marie. Please. They took him in—

Percy Hawkins, hometown hero," she said in staccato bursts. "They must have some damned good reason," she spewed, frantically pacing the floor.

"I'll try to get in contact with Mr. Alexander and have him call you as soon as possible."

"Thank you."

"You try to relax until we have all the facts. I'll get in contact with Mr. DuBois in Baton Rouge as well. Percy is one of his clients and I'm sure he'll want to help."

"Help? Help a murderer?"

"We don't know that, Michelene. I can't believe that Percy would do anything like this."

"Just please try to reach Chase," she said from between her teeth.

"I will."

Michelene hung up, turned and stared at the television. The damning image of Percy's near-perfect Nordic face seemed to taunt her from the screen.

In total disbelief, she sat down heavily on the couch. "How could you, Percy? Why?" she sobbed, covering her face with her hands.

—◆—

Then the phone calls started. One after another like a procession all asking the same thing, "Did you hear?" Martin, Paul and Kenny all called, wanting to lend their support. Several of her clients contacted her, each expressing their shock. Lisa's mother called and Michelene spent nearly twenty minutes trying to soothe her.

More than two hours later, a phone call came from Chase.

"Chase," she said, relief flooding her voice.

"Yeah, baby. I heard. It's all over the courthouse. Are you all right?"

"No. I'm not." She began to pace again.

"I'm going to try to get out there. The rain seems to be letting up some. But a lot of the roads are still flooded."

She shut her eyes in frustration, having totally forgotten about the rain, the second major deluge of the summer.

"I wish you would've come into the city and stayed with me when I asked."

"I can't conduct my business from your apartment," she snapped.

Chase took a breath, knowing that her caustic tone had nothing to do with him, but was Michelene's way of venting her pain.

"Just sit tight, baby. I'll get there."

Suddenly, her heart softened. The tight cramp in her stomach that once seemed to cut off her breath, slowly eased. She swatted away the line of tears that slid down her cheeks.

"Thank you," she whispered.

"Anything for you, baby. See you soon."

Chase hung up the pay phone in the hallway of the courthouse, then looked up and down the corridor. Everyone was buzzing with the news.

Lisa Renoir's murder was one of the most senseless crimes in the past thirty years, according to the police reports. Until today, there had been no suspect and no reasonable motive for her brutal death.

From his inside connection at the District Attorney's office, Chase knew that robbery was now ruled out and she had not been sexually assaulted. However, the full coroner's report was sealed and would remain that way until a trial was scheduled, and full evidence presented to both sides.

He could only imagine what Michelene was going through. Losing a friend was bad enough, then finding out that the alleged killer was someone you knew, defied explanation.

Slowly he bent and picked up his briefcase that sat at his feet. He had a very bad feeling about his case, and his instincts told him things would get much worse before they got better. And even as he stepped outside into the muggy afternoon heat, accompanied by a steady shower, the heavy premonition that sat in the center of his chest grew heavier.

The instant Chase returned to the office, he was dutifully informed by Marie that Lance had returned from Baton Rouge and wanted to see him right away.

"It's about Percy Hawkins," she said under her breath, her eyes wide and sad.

Chase nodded, slipped out of his trench coat and draped it over his arm.

"Thanks. Anymore updates since the news broke?" he asked, heading down the hall as he spoke.

"No. Mr. DuBois has been calling around trying to find out."

Chase nodded and continued down the hall until he reached Lance's closed door. He knocked, then stepped in without waiting for a response, an office practice that he secretly hated, except when it worked for his benefit. Like now.

Lance looked up when Chase came through the door and put his hand over the mouth of the telephone receiver. He waved Chase inside with his free hand and motioned for him to sit.

Lance swiveled his chair so that he faced the window, his back to Chase as he finished his hushed conversation.

Chase chose to stand, pacing the length of the Persian rug, head bent in concentration, hands slung in his pockets. The main thing on his mind was getting to Michelene and making sure she was all right. He hoped whatever Lance had to tell him was brief and to the point.

Finally, Lance finished up his conversation and turned his attention to Chase. He stood.

"I'm sure you heard that Percy Hawkins was picked up today in connection with Lisa Renoir's murder."

"Yeah. What else do we know?"

"That it's a ridiculous accusation first of all," Lance said angrily. "Percy could never do anything like that. And for what?"

"That's not much information, Lance," Chase said wryly.

Lance shot him a look from the corner of his eye and headed to the bar. "Bail's been set at two hundred and fifty thousand dollars."

Chase didn't comment, thinking it was quite low for a murder suspect. But he was sure the judge had taken Percy's notoriety into account.

"I want you to represent him."

"Lance, listen, he should really get someone—"

"You're the best at what you do, Chase, and Percy is a friend. I want him to have the best."

Chase tossed around the ramifications of taking on the case. It would certainly be a high-profile case, excellent public relations for the firm, and a major boost to his career. He could write his own ticket anywhere. But...

"I have to think about it," he finally said.

"There's nothing to think about. As your senior partner, I'm telling you to handle this case. Give it your best shot and get him off. He's innocent."

Chase frowned, staring hard at Lance. He'd never seen this side of him. Lance wasn't one who pulled rank to get what he wanted. He'd always been more diplomatic than that.

"Anthony Dunham is a friend of yours. He's personally handling this case. See if you can work something out."

"You're talking about a deal?" His uneasiness rose.

Lance set his drink down and braced his hands on his desk. "This is important. This town is going to be turned upside down if this goes to trial, which, unfortunately, it probably will." He exhaled a long breath. "Just go down there and arrange bail and get him out."

Chase shrugged into his coat. "I don't like how this thing feels, Lance. There's something you're not telling me. If I'm going to handle this case and win it, I need all the facts."

Lance turned his back and faced the window. "Our job is to give the best representation possible to our clients. That's our oath. Percy Hawkins needs a criminal defense attorney. You're the best one for the job. That's what you need to know." He paused a beat. "Give me a call when he's released, will you?"

Chase's jaw clenched. He turned and strode out. Stalking down the corridor, he stopped at Marie's desk.

"Marie, I need a favor."

"Certainly, Mr. Alexander."

"Please call Michelene. Tell her I got tied up and I'll be there as soon as I can."

"Of course. Is...everything all right, Mr. Alexander? You look upset."

He forced a smile. "Everything's fine."

Marie watched him as he hurried out.

※◆※

Getting the phone call from Marie was the last thing Michelene needed. Why couldn't Chase have called himself? she fumed. What had happened?

Restless and overwrought, she decided to take a long, hot bath. There was no telling when Chase would arrive, and maybe a sudsy soak would help to calm her frazzled nerves.

With her eyes closed, in a tub full of bubbles up to her chin, she kept seeing Percy's face as she did the last time he was in her house. Even in the hot water a sudden shudder ran through her body at the thought that a murderer had roamed freely through her home.

She thought she knew Percy. Could he kill someone? Was he capable of doing something so horrific? She'd prided herself on getting beneath the surface of people. Obviously she didn't know Percy at all.

But why? What reason would Percy Hawkins have to kill Lisa? They didn't even know each other. When it came time to make art purchases, Percy usually left the decision entirely in Michelene's hands. Although the three of them had grown up in Louisiana, they lived in separate towns. And Percy moved away right after high school.

She sighed. Maybe it was just a big mistake, like Marie said. People were falsely accused of things all the time. Still, it was too hard for her to imagine that the New Orleans police would arrest one of their great white hopes and accuse him of murdering a black woman if they didn't have some damned good reason.

It was after midnight by the time Michelene finally decided to give up on Chase and go to bed. She wasn't sure if what she felt as she slid between the sheets was anger or hurt.

The message from Marie was clear. It must have been awfully important for him not to show up and not call.

She flipped onto her side, staring at the iridescent red numbers on the bedside clock. Twelve forty-five.

She shut her eyes. Maybe when she opened them again this whole horrid series of events would have been a long nightmare.

The ringing of the downstairs doorbell infiltrated the heavy haze of her sleep. Blinking, Michelene listened closely. Maybe she was dreaming. No. There it was again.

Pulling herself out of bed, she snatched up her robe, slipping it over her red teddy as she hurried down the stairs.

"Chase." She fell into his arms. "I'm so glad you came," she whispered against his chest.

Tenderly he held her. "You shouldn't open the door like that without finding out who it is," he murmured into her hair.

She looked up into his eyes. "You're right. Especially now." She took his hand. "I'm just glad you're here. What happened?"

"We need to talk, Miki."

Her heart knocked in her chest, when she saw the serious expression in his eyes.

"Chase, what is it?"

"Let's talk inside."

—❦❖❦—

Michelene sat opposite him at the kitchen table in stunned disbelief, her outrage mounting by the second.

She shook her head as she spoke. "You can't be serious. How can you even think of defending him? He killed my friend."

"Michelene, listen. We don't know that."

"No! You listen." She slammed her palm down on the table. "That slime has been in my house, eaten my food, befriended me and then he strangled my best friend, squeezed the life out of her." Her voice began to break. "And you calmly sit there and tell me you're his attorney. My lover is defending my friend's murderer! Is that what you want me to listen to?"

"It's a lot more complex than that, Michelene, and you know it. I have a job to do, to defend my client to the best of my ability. Everyone is innocent until proven guilty."

Suddenly she stood. "Don't give me that legal bullshit. There comes a time when you have to look inside yourself to determine what's right, not what's dictated to you. I thought you were a better man than that. I was wrong about you, too."

"Michelene, this case isn't about us. It's about me doing my job. Protecting someone's rights."

"What about Lisa's rights?" She saw him flinch and almost enjoyed it. "You may think it's not about us, Chase, but it is. It's about who we are."

"Michelene, you're not being rational."

"Get out."

"What?"

"Leave now, Chase. And don't come back. I don't want to look at you and be reminded of what you're doing."

Chase stood and stared at her one last time. "You're making a mistake," he said, grabbing his coat and heading for the door. "Call me when you realize it."

"I hope you can sleep at night," she said to his back, and did everything in her power to keep the tears from falling.

Chapter Nine

And So It Begins

"Before we get started, Percy," Chase said as he paced the hi-gloss floors of Percy's palatial Algiers home. "You've got to get it in your head that I'm on your side. And the only way we can successfully defend you is if you tell me the truth. Understood?"

Percy, looking pale beneath his midsummer tan, absently nodded his head. He took a long swallow of bourbon from a crystal tumbler.

For a moment Chase's chest tightened. The glass reminded him of Michelene. She had a similar set in the antique china cabinet in her living room. Had she purchased these for Percy, as well?

"Did you kill Lisa Renoir?" Chase asked suddenly.

Percy snapped his blond head, his entire body seemed to coil. "No."

Chase watched him intently then slowly nodded his head. "That's where we start from—your innocence."

Percy took another gulp of his drink.

"Get rid of the drink. I want your head totally clear while we talk."

Reluctantly, Percy put the glass down on the mantelpiece, crossed the room and sat down on the six-foot modular couch.

Everything in Percy's home was hi-tech, straight out of the minds of the world's greatest designers. And Chase saw Michelene's touch everywhere.

"Where did you get the artwork?" Chase asked, staring at the Picasso on the pearl-gray wall.

"Michelene picked it up for me. I don't know a damn thing about art." Percy chuckled nervously. "She'd tell me a piece was good and I'd take her at her word."

"So you never had any direct dealings with Lisa Renoir?"

Percy swallowed. "No. Miki made all the transactions."

"Hmm. Had you ever met Lisa anywhere, at any time? Is there anyway to connect you with her?"

"No. I never met the woman."

"You're sure? Nothing at all will turn up later and surprise us?"

Percy looked away, unable to hold Chase's probing gaze. "No. Nothing."

"Then why were you seen leaving her house the night she was murdered, Percy?"

"I'm telling you, I wasn't there. It's a mistake."

"Do you have an alibi? Did anyone see you someplace else that night?"

"No. I was here. Alone. I was tired."

Chase shook his head, then lowered it as he spoke, crossing and recrossing the floor. "I need you to take some time and think, really hard. There has to be something that can prove where you were that night: a movie you watched, a casual visit to the liquor store, theater tickets, anything. Because I've got to tell you, you're the only suspect they have. An eyewitness places you at the scene and we have nothing to prove otherwise."

"I didn't do it! I didn't. I—" Percy stood and walked to the far side of the room.

"You what?"

"Nothing," he mumbled.

"Listen, Percy, you've got to be straight with me or I can't help you. It's as simple as that."

He turned, glaring at Chase. "Lance said you could get me out of this. And I'm paying you a helluva lot of my money to see that you do."

Chase picked up his briefcase. "I think you'd better find yourself another attorney." He walked toward the door.

"Wait."

Chase stopped, keeping his back to Percy.

"I'm...sorry. I know you're doing the best you can. But you've got to believe me, I didn't kill her."

Deliberately, Chase turned and stared at him for a long moment before speaking. "See what you can come up with for an alibi. We'll talk again in a couple of days."

Relief washed over Percy's face. Color came back into his cheeks. He nodded in assent. "Thanks."

"And stay put," Chase added, walking out to face the gauntlet of reporters that were camped out on Percy's front lawn. He hurried past them, waving them off. "No comment," he shouted, before sliding into his car and slamming the door.

—=◆=—

"Any calls, Marie?" Chase asked, returning to his office, hoping that Michelene had relented and decided to contact him.

"I left the messages in your box. Reporters have been calling all day."

"Hmm," he grumbled. "Is Lance in?"

"Yes, he just returned from court."

"Thanks." He headed down the corridor, dropped his things off in his office and walked across the hall to Lance's office.

"Come in," Lance called in response to the knock.

Chase opened the door and stepped inside.

"How'd it go?"

"Nothing new," Chase admitted on a note of exhaustion. "He's holding to his story. He doesn't know her, and he didn't do it."

"Of course. What did you expect him to say? The police have nothing but a half-wit eyewitness. That's it. They have nothing to go on."

Chase slung his hands in his pockets, lowered his head as he did when deep in thought. "There's something he's not telling me, Lance. My gut instinct tells me he's lying."

"Lying? Don't be ridiculous. Why would he lie?"

"If you were associated with a murder victim you might lie, even if you were innocent. You know the old adage, 'guilty by association.' Maybe he does know her, but since he can't prove where he was that night, he's denying everything."

"If Percy Hawkins said he didn't do it, he didn't," Lance stated.

Chase's gaze narrowed. "Why are you so damned sure?"

"Why aren't you?"

"Because I don't believe him."

The corner of Lance's mouth curved upward on the right side. "But you don't have to."

"I'll be in my office," Chase said, pushing down his brewing anger.

Lance stared at the closed door for several moments. As much as Chase may protest, he was the best. And if anyone could get Percy out of this mess, Chase could. He had to. There was too much at stake.

Michelene sat in front of her PC, transferring her daily information from the database to her palmtop.

Since Lisa's death, she'd virtually neglected her clients. Although they all empathized, saying they understood, she still had a business to run.

There were more than a dozen notices from the post office for packages that had to be picked up and delivered to her clients. But the truth was, her heart just wasn't in it. Part of her vitality, her zest was gone. She'd lost her dearest friend, her confidante, and she felt totally adrift. It would have been Lisa to whom she would have turned with her hurt over Chase. How twisted and ironic it was that the two people closest to her were linked in such a macabre way.

Finishing up her entries, she shut off her computer. She couldn't stay locked up in her house forever. And her clients deserved better than she'd been giving them. With that determination made, she got ready for her trip to the post office. Maybe just the act of getting out of the house and mingling with people, other than on the phone, would lift her from the malaise that consumed her.

Yes, that's exactly what she needed. Today would be a new beginning. Finishing her final makeup touches, she was about to get dressed when the phone rang. As much as today may be a new beginning, she really couldn't handle another complaint couched in the molasses-laced chatter she was sure to hear. She let the machine answer.

"Michelene."

Her heart stuttered.

"It's me Chase. Miki, if you're home, please pick up."

Emotion dictated that she run to the phone, snatch it up and tell the man she loved how much she missed and needed him, and how much she wanted to bridge the rift between them.

But she didn't.

"Michelene, please pick up."

Several moments later, she heard the dial tone.

Thoroughly shaken, she blindly finished dressing, all the while hearing Chase's voice ringing in her head. But she wouldn't give in. He had to see how wrong this was. How many more conflicts about his job would come between them in the future? She couldn't open herself to that. She couldn't. Pulling herself together, she headed downstairs, determined to move on with her day and with her life.

Just as Michelene was about to open her door to leave, the bell rang.

Her first prayer was that it was Chase, saying that she was right and taking the case was a mistake.

She peered through the peephole only to see two white men who were obviously police detectives judging from their off-the-rack suits and regulation black shoes.

Her heart beat a bit faster as she opened the door.

"Yes?" she smiled.

"Ms. Tyner?" the bigger of the two inquired.

"Yes."

"I'm Detective Thoreau, and this is Detective Paz. We'd like to ask you a few questions—about Lisa Renoir."

"Of course. Please, come in." She led them to the living room. "Can I offer you something cool to drink? Some iced tea?"

"That sure sounds fine," said Detective Paz, wiping his brow with a rumpled handkerchief.

When she returned with the tray of iced tea, Detective Thoreau was fingering a small marble sculpture on the coffee table. Detective Paz was looking over the Rembrant that hung over the fireplace.

"Gentlemen," she said announcing her arrival. She set the tray on the coffee table, poured two ice-loaded glasses and sat down.

The detectives retreated from their perusal and sat opposite her on the couch.

"We understand you and Ms. Renoir were very close."

"Yes. We were friends since childhood. We were more sisters than friends."

Paz jotted down something in his notebook.

"Then you would probably know as much about her as anyone?" Thoreau interjected.

Michelene smiled. "I would think so, yes."

"Was she seeing anyone—to your knowledge?" Paz asked.

Briefly she thought about the conversation she'd had with Lisa months ago, about the mystery man in her life, and how desperately Lisa wanted to keep the relationship under wraps. Suppose "he" was the one?

She started to tell them, but stopped. Lisa had entrusted her with that secret. They'd never betrayed each other in life and she wouldn't betray Lisa in death.

"No. There was no one that I know of," she said, which was partially true. She didn't know.

"Can you think of any reason why someone would want to

hurt her?" Paz asked, and before she could answer, Thoreau fired his question.

"Did she have any enemies? Maybe a disgruntled client?"

Slowly Michelene shook her head. "No. I can't think of anyone. Everyone loved Lisa. She was a wonderful person." Images of Lisa's smiling face as she moved about her gallery, showing pieces to clients for hours on end without complaint, going out of her way to get them exactly what they wanted. "The customer is the reason why I do this," Lisa once confided to Michelene. "Sure I love art, but what I really love is seeing someone's eyes light up when they can look beyond the canvas, beyond the texture of the sculpture to the passion that created it. That makes it all worthwhile." No, Michelene mused, Lisa didn't have any enemies.

"Did you know Ms. Renoir to travel to New York often, Ms. Tyner?" Thoreau asked, pinning her with his cool gray eyes.

She was thoughtful for a moment, trying to think of the countless places to which Lisa traveled. "I wouldn't say often. But she did go several times a year."

"Would you say two dozen visits in six months was often?" Thoreau volleyed.

Michelene frowned. "What are you getting at?" She glared from one to the other.

"Do you know what hotel she stayed in when she went to New York?" Paz quizzed.

Michelene shrugged slightly. "No."

"Did you ever accompany Ms. Renoir on any of these trips to New York?" asked Thoreau.

She didn't like the inflection of his tone. "I have my own business to run, Detective," she said fighting for control of her rising temper. She didn't like them. Didn't like their attitude, or what they were trying to imply.

"If there's something you want to say, Detectives, please say it. These innuendoes are quite tiresome."

The corner of Paz's thin mouth curved. "We're doing our job ma'am, trying to get to the bottom of a murder. The murder of your friend. I wouldn't think our questions would be 'tiresome,' as you put it, if you really wanted to see the culprit caught."

Michelene straightened, then stood, folding her arms beneath her breasts. "Anymore questions, gentlemen? I was on my way out of the door."

Paz snapped his notebook shut. Both detectives stood.

"You've been a great help, Ms. Tyner," Thoreau said, taking the last swallow of his iced tea and setting the glass back on the tray. "If you think of anything, even something small, please call me." He handed her his card.

Briefly she looked at it, but didn't respond. She led them to the door.

"When do you think her mother can get into her house...to get her things?" she asked once they were on the other side of the door.

"I'm sure someone will let her family know when it's okay. It should be soon," Thoreau said, giving her a sympathetic smile.

"*Merci.*"

"You have a good day, now, Ms. Tyner," Paz said, reaching for his handkerchief as soon as he stepped outside.

The detectives headed for their car, their conversation low and muffled.

Michelene slowly closed the door, shutting out the cloying heat, which still gripped the state in a chokehold. Good cop, bad cop, she thought absently.

Should she have told them about Lisa's beau? Thoughtfully she returned to the living room. Taking the tray, she took it to the kitchen, dumping the contents of the glasses into the sink and putting the glasses into the dishwasher.

Then the question arose: Where was he...whoever he was? And why hadn't he come forward?

The question plagued her as she drove into town. Maybe there was a way she could find out on her own. She certainly had enough connections. There had to be someone out there that knew something.

But as she drove passed the rows of overhanging cypress, brooding oak, heavy with Spanish moss, saw the sun dance off the rippling water of the stream, she was reminded of the thin line between life and death. Even as life continued, bloomed around, her Lisa's lifeless form blurred her vision and she thought about the hatred it must have taken to steal her life. And she knew, without a doubt, that she was entirely out of her league.

Chase was beside himself. Between the bad vibes he was getting about the Hawkins case, compounded with his hunger for Michelene, he felt as if his life was no longer under his control. The state of which he was totally unaccustomed.

He looked at the phone and thought about calling her again, telling her how bad he felt about the whole situation and that he didn't want to lose what they had because of a job.

But he didn't.

Instead he turned his concentration to the stack of documents on his desk. He flipped through the photos of the crime scene, looked at Lisa's bloated face, her life sucked from her.

From the photographs, it didn't look like a struggle had ensued. It was as if she'd been taken by surprise. There was no forced entry. Lisa Renoir knew her killer. She'd let him into her home.

Chase put the pictures aside and reviewed the reports from the policeman who had arrived at the scene first, and subsequent reports that included interviews with surrounding residents and the one eyewitness' testimony.

The full coroner's report was expected the following day. Maybe that would hold some clue.

Chase flipped the folder closed and pushed it across the desk, out of his line of sight.

He pressed the heel of his palms against his eyes, then slowly slid them across the stubble that peppered his jaw.

Maybe Michelene was right to put a halt to the relationship

when she did. It was obvious that their code of ethics would continually clash. If she wanted to walk out each time he took a case she didn't like, how long could they ever hope to last?

There was no future between them, he concluded. They were both two strong-willed, opinionated individuals who rarely, if ever, backed down.

But damn it, that didn't stop the ache in the pit of his belly, or fill the deep hole her absence had carved in his life.

He was better off before he met her, he decided. Before Michelene he didn't have to examine his feelings or rationalize his motives. Life was easy. It was his. And it was empty.

—✦✦✦—

It actually felt good being out again, getting her rhythm back, Michelene mused as she loaded her trunk with the packages from the post office. It was as if she'd stepped out of a dream. The shops, restaurants, boutiques and furniture stores clustered together on Magazine Street were overflowing with activity. Everything around her burst with brilliant energy. She could feel it flood her system as she drove through the streets around Jackson Square, passing wide-eyed tourists and slow-strolling inhabitants. Car horns honked, while music blared from barrooms and all-day all-nightclubs.

She actually missed it, she realized returning to her car after dropping off her last package—a set of imported linens she'd had shipped from China—at Ms. Daisy's house. Each year at Mardi Gras, Ms. Daisy threw one of the biggest masquerade parties in the county. Ms. Daisy swore the linens she'd purchased six months earlier "just wouldn't do."

Michelene smiled. Ms. Daisy was something else. Eighty years old and still feisty and going strong. She and her husband, Buford Longstreet, had gotten married right out of high school. According to Ms. Daisy they'd never spent a day apart in all those years.

What was it like to be with someone that long, Michelene wondered as she searched for a parking space. What was it like to love someone enough to want to spend the rest of your life with them?

Could it have been that way for her and Chase if she'd given it a chance? She knew she ached from wanting him, and felt empty, an almost starving sensation in the center of her stomach from missing him and the joy he brought to her life.

Was that how Daisy and Buford stayed together for so long because they never wanted to have that aching, empty feeling?

Easing into a parking space about a half block away from The Place, Michelene turned off the engine and stepped out of the car into the sticky, early-evening heat.

She wasn't quite sure why she'd decided to stop. All she knew was that she wasn't ready to go home. She wasn't ready to be alone again.

—≫◈≪—

"Hey there, Ms. Tyner," Bobby greeted, a full smile spreading across his redbone face. "Sure is good to see you again. You've been missed."

She forced a smile. "Thank you, Bobby. It's good to be back. Is Kenny around?"

Bobby peered over bobbing and weaving heads. Finally he pointed in the direction of the back dining room.

"There he is," he said. "He's coming this way."

Michelene leaned casually against the podium waiting for Kenny. Her eyes connected with his from across the room. She saw the slow smile move seductively across his mouth. His dark eyes sparkled in the candlelight. If there was one thing that was unquestionable about Kenny Loure, he was fine, even if he did get on her nerves at times and try to oversee her life.

"Cher," he crooned, kissing both of her cheeks. His gaze held hers for a moment. "Where is the laughter in your eyes, cher?" he asked, his voice holding a sincere note of concern.

"I'm fine. Really."

He put his arm protectively around her shoulders. "Do you

feel like company for dinner tonight?" he asked quietly, guiding her across the crowded floor to an intimate table in the back.

She looked up at him.

"I'd love to join you, Miki. If you don't mind."

A weak smile began to sprout. "Sure. I think I'd like that."

Kenny signaled for Chantelle, who sashayed over by the time Kenny and Michelene were seated.

"I'll be dining with Ms. Tyner tonight, cher."

Chantelle gave Michelene a quick cautionary look that held a measure of disdain. Then just as suddenly as it appeared, a practiced smile made its way across her chiseled features.

"Oui. Can I get you anything from the bar?" she asked, keeping her attention focused on Kenny.

"Two glasses and a bottle of champagne. We'll celebrate Michelene's return to The Place." He turned to Michelene, his eyes suddenly dark and probing. He took her hand. "How does that sound to you?"

Michelene nodded. "Fine."

Chantelle spun away in a huff, her contained fury as potent as a cheap perfume.

"Now, tell me, cher, how have you been? The truth."

She took a deep breath. "Not good. How's that for truth?"

"I know it must be hard," he said gently, stroking her hand with his thumb. "You and Lisa were so close. But it will ease with time."

"So I hear," she blew out.

"Has there been any more news? I can't believe that Percy Hawkins is accused of this." He shook his head in dismay. "For what reason?"

"It's the same thing I've been asking myself, Kenny."

They were quiet for a moment, each caught in their own thoughts.

"Where is your friend—Mr. Alexander? You two seemed...inseparable when you were here last."

Michelene looked away, her gaze landing on a couple locked in a slow drag in the middle of the floor.

"I'd rather not discuss it."

"It must be hard on the two of you with him defending Percy," he said trying to gauge the extent of the relationship by Michelene's response.

Slowly she removed her hand from his and folded hers on the tabletop. She leaned forward, her voice low and entreating.

"What part of 'I don't want to discuss it' didn't you hear, Kenny?"

A red tinge flushed his sandstone colored skin.

"You're right. I'm sorry." He waited a beat. "Please accept my apology." He gave her his best puppy-dog expression.

She didn't want to laugh, but she couldn't stop herself. "How can I be angry with you, Kenny?" she mumbled over her laughter.

"Now that's how I like to see you, my sweet Michelene, with a dazzling smile on your lips and a sparkle in your eyes. We will have a wonderful time tonight, I promise. How about if we start with shrimp remoulade or crab soup and then trout meuniere as the main course?"

"I'm starved already, cher."

As the evening wore on and the parade of patrons ebbed and flowed, dressed in everything and anything, Michelene found herself relaxing. The music from a Dixieland band kept the atmosphere lively all night.

She was glad she'd decided to stop by. Kenny was wonderful company, keeping up a steady flow of chatter, and doubling her over in laughter with ribald stories about his clientele.

"I thought she would swallow him whole," he said in a hushed voice. "The way she had her mouth all over him."

Michelene covered her mouth with her hand to stifle her laughter. "Kenny, you need to stop."

His eyes widened in mock offense. "But it's true. It wasn't human."

She tossed her head back and laughed some more. When she looked at him, his expression was soft.

"I promised you a good time, oui?"

"Yes, you did. And it's been wonderful," she added, taking a long sip of her champagne. She lost count long ago of how many glasses she'd consumed.

Michelene raised her arm to check her watch and realized that not only did her arm feel like lead, but that the numbers on her watched danced to the music of the band. She blinked trying to clear her head. Eleven fifteen faded in and out.

"I've got to...get home, Kenny."

"Of course." He stood, came around the table and held her chair.

When she stood, the room began to sway and she found herself leaning against Kenny to keep from falling.

He put his arm securely around her waist.

"The champagne really went to my head," she said slowly, taken aback by the effect of the alcohol.

"You can't drive, cher," Kenny warned.

"I can't very well stay here." She pressed her fingers to her eyes. Her head was beginning to pound. "I'll take a cab."

"Of course you won't. I'll drive you home." He sat her back in the chair.

"Just wait here a moment. I'm going to inform my staff that I'm leaving."

"What about my car?" she mumbled.

"I'll drive your car and take a cab from your house."

Michelene nodded her head and the room bounced up and down. She shut her eyes, feeling like a fool, but totally relaxed.

She must have dozed from the instant she sat down in the car, because when she opened her eyes, they were in her driveway and she had no recollection of the ride over.

She blinked, and felt her head clear. The short nap had definitely helped. She really felt silly now that her senses were back. She turned to Kenny.

"I'm so sorry to have you come all the way out here, Kenny," she apologized.

"Don't worry about it, cher. How are you feeling?"

She gave him a wan smile. "Much better."

"Good. Let's get you inside."

"At least let me make you some coffee with chicory for good measure," Michelene offered once they were inside.

"Consider my arm twisted. But let me do it. You relax."

"You twisted my arm," she sighed, plopping down on the couch. "Everything you need is in the kitchen."

Kenny walked out taking inventory of his surroundings. Michelene lived well. Just as well as some of her ritzy clients. But she worked hard and she was good at what she did, he realized, taking down the coffee from the cabinet. Michelene had brought him more business through the years than word of mouth.

He smiled to himself. Michelene Tyner was something special. Could she ever understand just how much he cared for her? He paced the spotless kitchen floor while he waited for the coffee to brew. It was pretty plain that Michelene and Chase were no longer an item, he concluded. He could tell by her expression and the way she refused to discuss him, which was a dramatic change since he'd last seen them together.

Maybe now she would see him for more than just a friend and business associate.

"Here we are," Kenny announced returning to the living room with a tray of coffee.

Michelene opened her eyes and smiled. "You really are sweet," she said dreamily.

"It's been a long time since I've been here, Michelene," he said, placing the tray on the coffee table. "Everything looks wonderful."

"Thank you." She reached for the coffee cup and Kenny

filled it for her. The potent brew quickly cleared the last of the cobwebs. "I'm really sorry about tonight, Kenny. It's been a while since I drank. It got me good."

He chuckled lightly. "Don't worry about it. It did you good. Made you smile."

"You made me smile," she returned, sipping her coffee.

"I'd do more than make you smile if you gave me half a chance, Miki. You know how I feel about you. Always have," he added gently.

"Kenny, you know I don't have those kinds of feelings about you. I care about you, but not like that. We talked about this."

"So this Chase is better, is that it?" His voice had hardened, and a sudden tightness gripped Michelene's chest.

"This is not about Chase and me."

"Isn't it? Isn't he the reason why you won't give me a chance?"

"Kenny, please. There was never anything between you and me long before I met Chase."

"You're not with him now. I told you he wasn't your type the minute I saw him." Kenny put his cup down, stood and came to sit beside Michelene on the loveseat. He took her chin between this thumb and forefinger, turning her face toward him.

"We can make magic together, Michelene. I know we can. I have enough love for the both of us."

"Kenny—I—"

"Are you in love with him? Is that it?"

For a moment she didn't answer, wasn't sure if she should, or what her answer really was. But then it was all so plain.

"Yes...I am. I love him, Kenny. I really do." And suddenly the weight that pressed down on her heart slowly eased.

Kenny pressed his lips together and nodded his head. "I guess that's pretty clear." He laughed half-heartedly. "How many times will I make a fool of myself over you, cher?"

"Never a fool, Kenny. Never." She tenderly brushed his lips with her fingertip.

"I should call that cab."

"I'll get the phone," she said leaving the room to retrieve the portable phone in the foyer.

"I hope he knows how lucky he is," Kenny said when she handed him the phone.

"I'm just happy I realized how lucky I am. And hope it's not too late."

Chapter Ten

What Goes Around

If it hadn't been so late by the time the cab service arrived to pick up Kenny, Michelene would have called Chase, especially if her head had been a bit clearer. What could be worst that groveling and having your words tumble all over one another? she concluded. Ultimately, she decided on a good night's sleep so that she could wake well rested and thinking clearly.

When she awoke the following morning, she was thrilled to see threads of sunlight streaming through the early-morning haze. She silently prayed that it wouldn't rain. She had plans. She wanted to walk along the Mississippi's banks holding Chase's hand while the orange ball of light that hung suspended in air slowly descended, radiating streams of luminous color across the water, only to be replaced by the bright white sphere that only lovers whisper about.

That's what she wanted to do today, she thought, feeling bright and alive as she stretched her arms high over her head before getting out of bed.

Padding barefoot across the pale-peach room, she entered the bath and turned the shower on full blast.

She'd been a fool, she realized, as she let the water pelt her flesh, the suds from the bath gel roll off her body. Michelene closed her eyes, raising her face to the water like the ancients held their faces to the heavens in prayer.

She loved Chase. She needed to tell him that. Convince

him of it. She'd allowed her personal feelings to come between them. She couldn't do that every time she disagreed with a case he took.

Shutting off the water, she stepped out of the beveled-glass stall and wrapped a thick peach and white striped towel around her dripping body. Her curls like tiny spirals of light glistened against her head. She wrapped a second towel around her hair to catch the water.

Entering her bedroom, Michelene checked the clock on the nightstand. Six A.M. She was chomping at the bit to call Chase, tell him how desperately she missed him and wanted to try to work things out between them. But she wanted everything right for that moment.

First, she'd get the perfect meal prepared, the perfect outfit ready, the music and lighting just right and then she would call him, use all of her feminine charms to convince him that with her is where he belonged.

She went down to the kitchen full of optimism and energy and began preparing the meal that she would offer in a pledge of peace to Chase.

Cutting up the vegetables for the gumbo she'd decided to fix, Michelene thought of her mother as she did many times when she cooked. Lena often said as she stood over the stove stirring and tasting, "The straightest road to a man's heart is through his stomach, or something like that." She'd laughed that musical sound that Michelene had copied and mastered making it her own. "Cooking is a way to clear your mind and put your heart and soul into what you're doing and sharing it with those you care about," she'd counseled.

Michelene remembered those words as the scents of peppers, onions, shrimp and vegetables began to fill the air. She hummed softly to herself, simply imagining sitting opposite Chase as they began the trek back toward each other.

Just as she was pouring the diced vegetables into the brewing pot, the phone rang.

"Good morning," she sang cheerily.

"Ms. Tyner?"

Michelene's brows crinkled. "Yes. Who's calling?"

"Ms. Tyner, this is Coleman Hunt, Ms. Renoir's attorney."

Her heart began to race with apprehension. "Yes. What can I do for you?"

"I don't know if you're aware of this, but Ms. Renoir left you as the executrix of her estate, which by my account is quite substantial."

Michelene's eyes rounded in alarm. "What are you talking about? I don't understand. What estate?"

"I'd like to discuss this with you in more detail. There are papers for you to sign and things I need to explain. I'd like to meet with you this morning. I know it's short notice but I'm scheduled to leave for California this afternoon, and I won't return for several weeks."

Michelene was in a state of shock. Her head couldn't seem to process the information. For a moment she thought it may have been the residual effects of all the champagne she'd consumed the night before.

"Is nine-thirty good for you, Ms. Tyner?"

"What?"

"Nine-thirty. Can you be at my office at nine-thirty?" he repeated in that tone you take with a child, slow and deliberate.

"Why are you calling me now?" she asked, regaining her mental balance, and beginning to wonder if this was some sort of hoax. "Lisa's been dead for weeks."

He cleared his throat. "I apologize for the delay in contacting you. I've been out of the country and only returned two days ago. I wanted to go over Ms. Renoir's affairs carefully before I spoke with you."

He sounds English, she thought absently, taking a breath. "Where is your office?"

She wrote down the address and phone number, registering the fact that his office was in Baton Rouge, a nice drive on any other day.

"I'll be there," she said finally.

"And Ms. Tyner, I'd appreciate it if you didn't discuss this with anyone until after we've talked."

The sound of dial tone hummed in her ear.

Michelene leaned against the counter and stared at the piece of stationery with the phone number and address. As far as she knew, Lisa was doing well financially, but by no means did she ever discuss a "substantial estate." Michelene's stomach began to flutter. What was going on? And why couldn't she talk to anyone?

Michelene glanced at the wall clock. Seven thirty. By rote she compared it to her wristwatch. If she hurried she might get to Mr. Hunt's in the vicinity of nine-thirty.

She turned off her pot and with that, realized that her best-laid plan for Chase was temporarily derailed.

With disappointment slowing her steps, she went upstairs, picked out a navy blue single-button pantsuit and proceeded to get dressed, and all the while her anxiety mounted over her impending meeting with Mr. Hunt.

Did she need her own lawyer to be present, she wondered, stepping into navy pumps. After all, the man did say there were papers for her to sign.

Contemplating a moment, she decided to give her attorney a call just to be sure. As she reached for the phone on the nightstand, it rang in her hand.

"Hello?"

"Michelene?" the frail voice asked and she instantly knew the identity of the caller.

"Mrs. Renoir. How are you?"

Celeste Renoir sniffed. "The police said I could collect Lisa's belongings...from her house."

A sinking sensation swept through Michelene's center. Although she knew this day was inevitable, she resented its arrival. It was just another reminder of Lisa's absence from their lives.

Michelene exhaled a long, sad breath. "When did you want to go?"

"This morning."

"Today?"

"I have to get this over with. I can't stand the thought of having to deal with it some other day. I want to put this behind me."

"I understand."

"Would you pick me up? I'm not up to driving."

Michelene quickly weighed her options. She didn't have any. There was no way she'd disappoint Lisa's mom. Maybe it wouldn't take long and she could still get to her mysterious appointment with Mr. Hunt without keeping him waiting too long.

"Of course, Mrs. Renoir. I'm already dressed and I can be there in twenty minutes." If she broke the speed limit.

"Thank you," she breathed in relief. "I'll see you shortly."

Michelene hung up the phone. Had the attorney spoken to Lisa's mother? Apparently not. The more she thought about it, she knew Lisa's mother knew nothing about any estate.

Perhaps she should have told her about the impending meeting with Mr. Hunt. But it was probably best to follow his advice and not say anything until she found out exactly what was going on.

If things got too dicey, she'd call her attorney from Mr. Hunt's office. With that decided, she collected her purse, cell phone and palmtop and dashed out. Maybe by some miracle, she could actually get everything done.

When Michelene arrived at Mrs. Renoir's home, she was shocked to see how fragile she'd become in just a few short weeks. Lisa's death had taken a physical toll on Celeste Renoir.

"Thank you so much for coming, dear," Celeste said, laboriously getting into the passenger seat of the Benz.

Michelene leaned over and kissed Celeste's cool brown cheek. "Please, don't mention it. Anything for you." She pulled off and headed in the direction of Lafayette, followed the road to Teshe, the state's largest bayou, just beyond Acadia where Lisa's home was tucked away among the Spanish moss and sluggish waters of the bayou.

"Never could understand why that child moved all the way out here," Celeste said almost to herself as the towering cypress offered canopies of green shade against the already blazing sun.

They passed several small villages that rose out of the water on stilts, and moored fishing boats could be seen every so often dotting the water.

As they drew nearer to Lisa's hideaway, surrounding homes grew more scarce and Michelene was overwhelmed by a sudden wave of sadness imagining Lisa's terror and no one to hear her screams.

When they finally pulled up in front of Lisa's house, a one time plantation that had been cut down and restored, they both became paralyzed by the sight of the yellow tape that now hung in pieces around the perimeter of the house.

For several moments they sat in the car staring at the house, trapped in their own visions of happier times, now forever marred.

Celeste took a shaky breath, her small body vibrating with the effort. "I should get this over with," she said.

Michelene nodded, got out of the car, came around and opened Celeste's door. Together they walked down the short, shaded path, braced on either side by rich grass and well-tended hedges that were just beginning to show signs of neglect, until they reached the front steps.

It was only three steps to the door, Michelene thought, holding Celeste's arm, but it felt like three hundred.

"I have a key," Celeste mumbled, her hand shaking as she stuck the key in the lock.

They stepped inside, and an uneasy feeling of budding fear built like a match carelessly tossed on a mattress to smolder.

The air inside was close, tight and a haze, real or imagined hovered in the air, mingling with the scent of things unseen.

Michelene reached for the light switch on the wall and the front room was bathed in soft white light chasing the ghosts away.

It felt as if at any moment, Lisa would glide down the spiral staircase and greet them. But she never would again. And they both felt the pain of that realization at the same moment.

Celeste squeezed Michelene's arm more in reaction to the reality than for support. "She's really gone," Celeste said quietly. She walked farther into the house, lovingly touching objects as she passed. Then suddenly she began to cry and turned to Michelene. "Would you mind terribly if I did this alone?" she asked as silent tears slid down her cheeks. "I know I got you all the way out here...but..."

Michelene came to her side, putting her arm around Celeste's shuddering shoulders. "Please, Mrs. Renoir, you don't have to explain. But are you all right? Are you sure you want to do this alone?"

Celeste nodded her head.

"I'll come back for you in a few hours. I have an appointment in Baton Rouge."

Celeste pressed her trembling lips together. "Thank you," she whispered. "Lisa was lucky to have you as a friend."

"I was lucky to have her," Michelene replied. She patted Celeste's arm. "I'll see you in a few hours."

—◦◦◈◦◦—

It took Michelene close to an hour to return to the city. She'd called Mr. Hunt's office, en route, to inform his assistant of her delay. By the time she arrived, it was after 10:30.

"Mr. Hunt will be with you directly," the white-haired assistant said in a slow drawl, when Michelene arrived slightly harried.

"Thank you."

"Just have a seat," the woman said, indicating a straight-backed Queen Anne chair in the far corner of the dimly lit space.

Michelene made her way to the chair and sat, giving the room a cursory glance as she did, and quickly concluded that

Mr. Hunt's legal office needed a full remodeling job.

Shortly, a rather tall, slenderly built, middle-aged white man, came through a side door.

"Ms. Tyner," he said, extending his long piano-fingered hands. "Thank you for coming on such short notice. Please, come inside."

He led her into his office, which was a larger version of the reception area.

"Would you like some coffee, juice?"

"No. Thank you," she said, taking a seat on the opposite side of the square wooden desk.

"I'm sure you've been wondering why all the cloak and dagger." He smiled benevolently at her.

She didn't answer.

He reached for a thick manila folder on his desk and pulled it toward him. Retrieving a pair of half-glasses from the breast pocket of an apparently well-made gray suit, he slid them onto the tip of his nose, and flipped the folder open.

"To begin, Ms. Renoir's assets are somewhat in the neighborhood of a bit over two million dollars—"

"What?" Michelene's heart began to hammer.

"Please, let me continue. That includes the gallery and its contents, her house and its contents, selected pieces of art, her car and some property she purchased in Algiers."

Michelene could have sworn she was hearing things. Nothing was making sense. Everything this man was saying was running around in her head like a cat chasing its tail. She'd always thought that Lisa was renting the gallery space, not that she owned it and everything in it. Sure she'd been aware that Lisa had acquired some exquisite art pieces of her own over the years, but she'd never thought about how much they were worth. How could she have afforded to do all this, and why hadn't she ever told her?

Michelene was beginning to feel sick. Property in Algiers? Why?

"Of course everything will have to be appraised," he was saying when she caught up with the conversation.

She looked at him as if seeing him for the first time. Her throat was tight. Who was Lisa Renoir?

"I'd like to wrap this up as soon as possible. According to the stipulations of Ms. Renoir's will, you are now the sole owner of all her assets, to do what you will with them."

Michelene couldn't talk. She didn't know what to say.

"Would you mind signing here, please?" He slid a legal-looking paper across the desk.

Michelene stared at it blindly. "What is this?"

"Just a statement from my office saying that I've advised you of the contents of the will on this day. You will have to get a lawyer to iron out all of the particulars for you, help you to decide what you want to do with the property. If you'll give me their name, I can forward the documents over to them. Or if you prefer, you can take them now."

She swallowed, scribbled her signature on the statement and handed it back. "I'll take them with me."

"Certainly." He leaned over and pressed the intercom.

"Yes, Mr. Hunt."

"Please prepare the documents for Ms. Tyner. She'll be taking them with her on her way out."

"Of course."

He stood. Michelene did the same.

"If there's anything else I can do for you, Ms. Tyner, please call me," he said, walking her to the door. "I know this must be difficult and quite a shock."

Suddenly, she stopped and turned to face him. "How long have you known Lisa?" she asked, almost afraid of the answer.

He smiled. "I've been Lisa's attorney for about ten years now."

With the envelope tucked under her arm, somehow without really seeing, Michelene found her way out of the building and to her car. Everything she'd thought, believed to be true for years, was one big lie. Lisa was the one person in whom she trusted unquestionably, and now she had no clue as to who Lisa really was. Her reality was beginning to crumble around her.

For several moments Michelene sat in her car, numb. How could she drive back to Lisa's house and face her mother, knowing what she did? And what about Lisa's mother? Did she know about any of this? Did she know her daughter? Michelene covered her face with her hands.

When she removed her hands and looked out the window, Chase was crossing in front of her with his arm snugly around Sylvia Tanner's waist.

Chapter Eleven

Nothing Is What It Appears

It could have been any number of things, Michelene thought as she drove back to Lisa's house. There had to be some explanation as to why Chase was all hugged up with Sylvia Tanner.

But she couldn't think of one. Especially with her heart aching as if it truly wanted to break. Her thoughts scattered, overloaded with the events of the day. But with every blink of her eye, she saw Chase and Sylvia.

Did Paul know that his fiancée was being squired around town with her ex-boyfriend? How could Chase do something like this? Did what they have mean so little that at the first opportunity he'd find his way into someone else's arms?

Hurt and disappointment gave way to anger. To think that she was on the threshold of groveling, apologizing, imploring to get him back into her life. He wasn't giving her the time of day.

Fine. If that was the way things were, the hell with him. She didn't want an explanation. At this point he could tell her anything. He was probably seeing Sylvia all along, making fools of her and Paul.

She had other things to occupy her mind. First and foremost what to do about her meeting with Mr. Hunt. But even as she drew closer to Lisa's house, she could not deny the pain that had found a home in the center of her being.

Lisa's mother was sitting on the veranda by the time

Michelene pulled into the driveway. It appeared as if Celeste was totally unaware of Michelene's arrival. Her gaze was focused beyond a point that Michelene could see.

Cautiously Michelene approached and spoke in soft tone. "Mrs. Renoir." Gently she touched Celeste's shoulder.

Watery eyes looked up at Michelene's face. A shaky smile inched across her mouth then quickly disappeared.

"Hello, dear."

Michelene looked around. "Are you...ready?"

"Yes. I put a few things in boxes. They're in the house," she answered in a faraway voice.

"You sit here and I'll put them in the car."

Celeste nodded and continued staring off into space.

There were four large boxes packed with what, Michelene didn't know. She looked around the house and saw that the photographs that always sat on the throne on the mantle were gone. The porcelain figures and carved wooden statues were gone as well. Giving the boxes a quick look, she saw Lisa's silver, several of her favorite dresses, a photo album and an assortment of other mementos. One by one, she took the boxes to the car.

Slightly winded, she came back for Mrs. Renoir. "All the boxes are in the car," she said softly. "Are you ready?"

Celeste sighed heavily, stood without a word and moved toward the car.

Michelene took a last look at the house, locked the door and they headed off.

For the hour it took them to return to Mrs. Renoir's home, Michelene didn't utter a word. She wasn't sure what to say to the woman who'd lost her daughter. In reality what could she say that could possibly make things any easier: that she'd inherited all of Lisa's worldly possessions, that Lisa was a very rich woman and neither of them knew anything about it, that she'd been seeing a strange man for months and didn't want anyone to know? Were those the things she wanted to talk to Mrs. Renoir about? Would she be able to shed some light on the mystery of Lisa's life?

Finally, the hour of silence was over.

"We're here, Mrs. Renoir. I'll take the boxes up for you."

"No. I packed them for you. There's nothing of Lisa's that I want. I'd like to remember her the way I thought she was." She turned sad eyes on Michelene. "Do with them as you wish."

Confusion danced across Michelene's face. "I...don't understand."

Celeste patted Michelene's hand. "Don't try to, dear. Move on with your life. Lisa was a wonderful girl and I loved her dearly, but over the last year—" She sighed and opened her door. "Thank you." Celeste shut the car door and went inside her house, never looking back.

Mentally and emotionally drained, Michelene stood in her living room staring at the damning boxes, anxious on one hand to view the contents and terrified on the other. What secrets were held in the boxes, and did she really want to know?

She sat down on the couch, draping her arms across her thighs. Finally she pulled one box toward her and began sifting through the contents.

For the most part it was much as she expected, photos, some jewelry. At the bottom of the first box, there was a sealed manila envelope. With much trepidation, Michelene ripped it open. Airline ticket stubs.

Her pulse began to pound and a surge of heat swept through her. New York, California, Italy, Mexico. The list went on. At first she didn't want to speculate. Maybe it was a coincidence that the detectives had asked her about Lisa's trips.

Michelene shoved the tickets back into the envelope as if the action would make the reality go away. She ran a hand through her tight, damp curls. She didn't like the feeling she was getting. Not at all.

Forcing herself to continue she went through the next box,

finding more of the same and with each moment the tightness in her chest increased. But in the last box, the final item made her heart stand still and the one thing that had hung in the back of her mind, never spoken out loud screamed its truth.

She pulled the scarf from the box, pressed it to her face and cried.

—❖—

"Do you have an appointment?" the receptionist asked when Michelene requested to see Anthony Dunham.

"No. I don't. But if you'd just tell him Michelene Tyner is here, I'm sure he'll see me," she said, trying to stay calm. "Please. I'll wait." She gave the woman her best smile, crossed the small waiting room space and sat down on a low, brown leather couch. She crossed her legs, swinging her right one while she waited.

Casually she watched the Tyra Banks look-alike speak softly into the telephone. When she finished she made eye contact with Michelene. "Mr. Dunham said it would be about fifteen minutes. He's on a business call."

"Thank you." Michelene reached for a magazine on the gleaming cherry wood table and thumbed through the current issue of Essence.

It was more like a half hour by the time Anthony entered the waiting room. She'd gone through every magazine on the table twice.

"Michelene." Anthony walked up to her, the picture of perfection from the top of his expertly styled hair to the gleam on his seven-hundred-dollar shoes. Anthony was never one to scrimp on clothes and personal pleasures, that was one thing Michelene remembered about him, that and his appetite for rough sex. She swallowed, pushing back the dark memories. This wasn't about rekindling something that should have never been. This was about bringing some justice.

Michelene stood and extended her hand.

"Since when do we shake hands, cher," he said in that

deceptively crooning voice that could travel the length of your body in the blink of an eye. He kissed her right cheek, her left, then held her at arm's length by her shoulders. "You look beautiful as always. To what do I owe the pleasure?"

"I need to talk with you, Anthony."

He frowned, his creamy caramel complexion darkening slightly. "Come in my office."

They passed the receptionist. "Stacy, no calls," he instructed.

"Yes, Mr. Dunham."

Michelene could feel Stacy's eyes following them even beyond the closed door.

"Can I get you anything?" Anthony asked once they were inside his office.

"No. Thanks."

Anthony took a seat on the couch and Michelene sat beside him at a discreet distance. He leaned his elbow on the back of the couch and rested his chin in his palm, one of the many tactics he used to lull the unsuspecting into a sense of security. Michelene had seen it all before.

"So, tell me, what can I do for you?"

"It's about Lisa's case."

He sat back a moment. "You know I can't discuss a case with you, Michelene—"

"I know. That's not why I'm here." She took a breath and reached into her purse, pulling out the scarf. "I came about this."

He chuckled. "I'm pretty damned good at what I do, cher, but reading minds and symbols is even a bit much for me."

"This belonged to Lisa."

"And—"

"Percy Hawkins purchased it for her."

He looked at her for a moment, trying to see beyond the words. "Why are you so sure? There has to be hundreds of scarves like this one," he said holding it up for examination.

"There aren't. I had it designed specifically for Percy. It was sent from Italy."

"You're sure?"

"Absolutely. I'd stake everything on it."

Anthony was thoughtful for a moment. "This would link him to Lisa," he muttered to himself. He blew out a breath. "It may be just what we've been looking for."

Michelene's heart started to thunder in her chest.

Anthony's gaze zeroed in on her. "Would you be willing to testify?"

"I'd be willing to do anything to see Lisa's murderer brought to justice."

"Even fabricate evidence?"

She sprung from her seat. "You know me better than that, Tony. If Percy Hawkins lied about knowing Lisa, what else is he lying about? I know this is the scarf I purchased for him and he gave it to Lisa. It was among her things that her mother and I picked up from her house."

"All right, all right. Take it easy. I just don't want to jump the gun and blow this thing."

She folded her arms and waited.

"I'll check it out."

"Thank you." She picked up her purse from the couch. "Will this be enough?"

"It's a start. There could be several explanations."

"There aren't. Believe me."

"Is there more to this, Miki?"

She sat back down, contemplating revealing more, then realizing if she was going to go all the way, she had to spill it all.

With quiet deliberation, she told him all about Lisa and her mystery man and how Percy was always buying things for a woman. She concluded by telling him about the stack of airline tickets that she'd found in an envelope in one of the boxes from Lisa's house.

"If we could connect the airline tickets to times that Percy was also in those places, it would make for a tighter case. Where are they?"

She reached into her purse and pulled out the envelope,

handing it to Anthony.

"You've been very busy. Maybe I should get you on my investigating team."

"This is not the kind of job I'd ever enjoy," she said. "I'd better go."

He walked her to the door. "Your boyfriend isn't going to be too pleased that you've gone over to the other side," he taunted.

She turned and faced him, her expression resolute. "He's anything but my boyfriend." With that she walked out, her heart heavy but her mind finally clear.

Chapter Twelve

A Reason for Everything

Michelene hadn't returned any of his calls, Chase realized, stuffing the last of his court papers into his briefcase. He thought he could push her to the back of his mind, occupy the missing space with work, the new case, the fever of the hunt. He couldn't. And he didn't know what it was he felt anymore: disappointment or anger at her and at himself. And adding to his mounting agitation was the impromptu visit by Sylvia Tanner that afternoon.

Sylvia was the last person he expected to see, especially under the circumstances. Although he and Sylvia had parted company somewhat amicably, he'd never thought she'd seek him out. She insisted during the entire, bizarre conversation, that she was speaking with him on behalf of "a friend." He knew better. Sylvia Tanner had gotten herself into something much deeper than she'd ever bargained for.

What to do about it was now his major concern, and like it or not, Michelene was the one person who might be able to answer some of the questions that were begging to be answered, and possibly get his client off. A possibility that he knew Michelene wouldn't be amenable to.

Michelene stared at her television, unseeing, already curled up in bed at the ungodly hour of eight p.m. Exhaustion had taken hold of her like a bad case of the flu, leaving her feeling weak and listless. Yet, her mind wouldn't stop running, refusing to let sleep capture her. *Lisa, murder, large sums of money, the scarf, airline tickets, Chase, Sylvia, Chase...Chase.*

She squeezed her eyes shut and slid further beneath the cool pearly white satin sheets.

Everything was coming apart. She didn't know which way to turn. All upon which she'd built her foundation of truth, were lies, crumbling beneath her and she had nothing of substance to latch on to.

Lisa and Percy. How? Why? Lisa was her dearest friend. But Lisa led a life she knew nothing about, whispered things in the dark she would never hear and somehow that other life had been the cause of her death.

Now in retrospect, she could understand Lisa's unwillingness to divulge the identity of her lover. It may be the nineties, but this was the south—the deep south—and interracial relationships were still frowned upon no matter who you were.

A rush of sadness flowed through her, filling her chest. How lonely Lisa must have felt loving a man she couldn't acknowledge and who wouldn't acknowledge her, watching him from a discreet distance and knowing what was in her heart. Loving was difficult enough in the best of circumstances, Michelene mused philosophically, but compound that with the weight of racial hatred and superstardom and you had tragedy at your doorstep.

Just weeks earlier, the world stood in open-mouth horror when an innocent black man was dragged to his death by a band of white hate mongers. Then watched silently, shaking their collective heads at the parade float filled with civil servants in blackface. Even at the highest levels of government, its members were clamoring for the rollback of affirmative action. We've been equalized.

Had Percy suddenly become a part of that silent rage? What had Lisa done to cause Percy to murder her—be born black? What secret did she have that he was afraid she'd reveal? Were they involved in something that had gone sour? And how in heaven's name did Lisa amass so much money?

Questions. Questions. Michelene's head pounded. Gently she massaged her temples, then the tender bridge of her nose. Between the thumps in her head, she thought she heard the doorbell. Maybe it was only the television, she prayed, refusing to come out from the cushiony safety of her cocoon. There it was again.

Groaning, she sat up just as the phone rang.

"Damn. What is this?" She snatched up the portable phone, grabbed her robe and ran downstairs. The bell pealed again.

"Hello?"

"Ms. Tyner, this is Detective Paz."

She stopped short on the staircase. "Yes?" Her heart thumped.

"Some information has just become available to us, Ms. Tyner, and I was hoping you would be willing to come down to the station tomorrow morning to discuss it," he drawled.

She took the final three steps. "What information?"

"I'd rather discuss this with you in person, Ms. Tyner. I could send a car for you if that would help."

"That won't be necessary," she said feeling breathless. "What time?"

"Anytime before noon. If that's convenient for you."

"I'll be there." She walked across the foyer to the front door.

"Thank you, Ms. Tyner. I'll be expecting you tomorrow. Good night." He clicked off.

Michelene's hands shook when she depressed the Off button with one hand and opened the door with the other.

"Chase!"

"I was about to give up," he said, his voice as soft and gentle as a spring breeze.

For several seconds they simply stared at each other, their insides full and tight with the sight of each other, realizing just how much they'd missed.

132

Michelene's throat constricted. "I—"

"I missed you." There, he'd said it. "I can't think. I don't want this case, any case to come between us, Michelene. Just talk to me."

She reached out and caressed his face with the tips of her fingers, pushing aside the scene with him and Sylvia. He was here now, with her. "I missed you, too," she confessed, her eyes raking over his face. She took his hand and led him inside, through the foyer, up the stairs into her bedroom.

No sooner than the door shut behind them, did Chase pull Michelene into his arms, his mouth, his body hungry for her— for the taste of her, the feel of her against him. Currents of white heat shot through his body as his hands glided along the silky fabric of her gown, lifting it to find the butterscotch velvet beneath.

"Michelene," he groaned against her neck, nibbling the tender skin.

She emitted a soft sigh, allowing the warmth to push away the cold emptiness she'd felt.

Chase slid the robe from her shoulders and lifted the baby pink gown over her head. A ragged sigh from deep inside of him filled the charged air at the sight of her. He felt transfixed as always when he looked at Michelene. She was perfect, from the tips of her firm breasts, right down to the faint stretch marks that touched her hips, giving her body character, a sense of reality.

A slow, seductive smile traveled across her unpainted mouth as she held Chase in place with just a look while she unfastened the buttons to his blue Oxford shirt, unbuckled the belt that cinched his waist and unzipped his pants, letting them pool around his ankles.

The navy silk boxers—oh, yes she remembered well when she'd purchased them for him—did little to hide the firmness of his brown thighs or the dangerous erection that throbbed beneath.

She moved closer, pressing her naked body against him, spiraling his desire for her, and hers for him. He stepped out of his pants, and pulled his shirt from his body, nearly ripping it in the rush of urgency that had rapidly taken control of his body. Heat swirled around them. He slid his hand between her pliant thighs, searching for and finding the welcoming wetness there.

Michelene trembled when his finger stroked the bud, making it bloom like a flower needing water.

Chase encircled her waist, probing deeper with the tip of his finger, his tongue delving into her mouth, in and out, tasting her lips, exploring her depths.

She touched him then, and felt him shudder as she rubbed her finger across the tip of his erection.

"Michelene," he gasped.

Her heart raced frantically. "Make this better," she said in a hot whisper.

"My pleasure," he said taking her to bed.

⊷⊰⊙⊱⊶

As they lay in each other's arms, legs entwined, fingers interlaced, bodies still damp with the telltale sheen of hot loving, they whispered in the dark, words that only lovers share: beautiful...always...I'm sorry...wonderful...so happy...I'm yours.

Chase brushed a damp curl from Michelene's forehead, running a finger across her smooth brows. "You're incredible," he uttered.

"I couldn't be by myself, Chase. You touch a place inside me I didn't think was reachable. When I'm with you, I feel complete. I didn't realize how much a part of me you'd become until—"

"Let's not go back there. This is about moving forward, baby. You and I, together, whatever it takes. You've got to have faith in me and not bolt every time things get shaky. If I know I have you at my side, hey, I can handle anything, no matter how grim things get. But I need to know you're there for me."

She let out a long breath. "I was so wrapped up in my personal hurt, my feelings, I didn't think about you. All I could see was Lisa—gone—and you representing the man accused of killing her. It didn't matter to me that you were doing your job, just that I was hurt. I felt betrayed somehow."

He kissed her head. "I know, baby. I know. But it's not personal. We can't let it be personal, or it'll destroy us. This is the first time in longer than I can remember that I want someone to be a part of my life—a real part. I look forward to a future with you in it. I didn't realize that until I met you, I was dead inside. You revived me, brought me back to life. I don't want to lose that."

"It'll be better this time, I promise."

He smiled. "I'm going to hold you to that."

She snuggled against him. "I'm glad you didn't give up on me," she whispered.

"I thought you'd given up on me."

"I'll tell you a secret," she said, a new lightness in her voice. "I was going to come to you today groveling, begging you to forgive me."

He leaned his head back to look at her to see if she was serious. She was. "Why?"

"Because...I love you. I never had the chance to say it, but I do. I love you, Chase, with all my heart."

Slowly he lowered his head. "I've waited to hear you say those words."

His mouth covered hers in a tender, soul-stirring kiss, sealing their pact. "I love you, too, baby. Believe that."

As Michelene arched her hips to meet him, and felt the power of him enter and fill her, she knew that not only was her body committed to this man, but her heart—totally.

"I know this may not seem like the best time to talk about this," Chase said with hesitation. "But something came up today that I hope you may be able to shed some light on."

Michelene turned on her side to face him, running her hand along his bare arm. "What is it?"

"Sylvia Tanner came to see me today. We had lunch."

"Oh." She could have gotten an award for her noncommittal performance.

"She said she was talking to me for a friend, but I have serious doubts about that."

Michelene's stomach began to seesaw.

"What did she say?"

"She said what if someone was moving stolen merchandise through a third party, but they didn't know the merchandise was stolen when they passed it along."

Her heart started to hammer like a carpenter knocking in that last stubborn nail...boom, boom, boom.

"What did you tell her?"

"That the person could be considered an accessory, if the prosecutor could somehow prove that the person knew what they were doing."

Michelene stopped stroking his arm. She knew in the pit of her soul that the worse was right around the curve of the next sentence.

"How much do you know about Lisa's business dealings? Where did she make her purchases?"

"Why would you make any kind of connection between Lisa and Sylvia's question?" she asked stalling for time.

"I just find it too much of a coincidence that this major investigation is going on, we have no probable cause for Lisa's death and Sylvia shows up out of the blue with this loaded question. It doesn't take a genius to put two and two together."

If they were going to move forward she had to be upfront with him. She took a long pause, then began retelling the events of the day, ending with the call from Detective Paz.

"You gave the scarf to Anthony?" he asked incredulously.

"What choice did I have? I couldn't very well bring it to you. You're defending him."

"So now Tony has the piece of evidence to link Percy to Lisa."

"Something would have turned up eventually, Chase," she said in her defense, momentarily remorseful about her actions, even knowing it was the right thing to do. "It was bound to. The police already know about the airline tickets. Even as inept as they seem it wouldn't be long before they pieced the puzzle together."

Chase blew out a breath from between his teeth. "He lied to me. I always knew he was lying, I just didn't know why."

"But if you knew he was lying, how could you defend him? That's what I don't understand."

He pulled up the sheet to cover her. "I didn't want the case to begin with," he confessed. "I felt I was too close to it. With Lisa being your friend—"

She frowned. "If you didn't want it, why did you take it?"

"Let's say I wasn't given much of a choice. I'm a partner in the law firm. The decision was made by Lance, my senior partner. Percy Hawkins is a long-time friend of Lance's and a client. There was nothing I could do."

Michelene looked away. "I didn't know."

"You didn't give me a chance to explain. But that's not the issue. Percy lied to me for a reason. There's some reason why he doesn't want anyone to know he was in a relationship with Lisa."

"It's pretty obvious. He's a white man having an intimate relationship with a black woman in the deep south. Compound that with his admitting to knowing her, they may find a way to tie him to the crime just to teach him a lesson."

"Not if he didn't do it."

"It happens every day, Chase. You said so yourself. People are locked up all the time for crimes they didn't commit."

"True, but when was the last time you ever heard of a white superstar athlete doing any kind of time for any kind of crime?"

She didn't answer.

"I rest my case." He shook his head. "There's more to this than just Percy trying to hide a relationship with a black woman. And he's going to tell me what it is."

"What will Anthony do?"

"Probably press for an indictment and move that we go to trial, something I was hoping to avoid."

"Do you think that Percy did it, Chase?"

"No. I don't. I never did. But he's guilty as hell about something. It's just not Lisa's murder. Of that, I'm sure."

They were both quiet until Michelene finally spoke several minutes later.

"I wonder what the police want to question me about," she said, a tight, tremulous edge to her voice.

"I'd say they want to question the sole beneficiary of Lisa Renoir's estate, and how you've benefited from her demise."

Chapter Thirteen

Cause and Effect

"You need to give your attorney a call, Michelene," Chase advised, pushing his arm through the sleeve of his shirt.

"You really think so?" She was getting nervous.

"It'll do you more good than harm. You don't want them coercing you into anything." He began buttoning his shirt, smiling slightly at the sight of a missing button, remembering how it had come off. "Who's your attorney?"

"Pamela Mitchell."

His brows knitted a moment. "She's a corporate attorney, isn't she?"

"Yes. The only reason I've ever needed a lawyer was for business."

"Hmm." He buckled his belt. "She'll have to do."

"That's reassuring," she said drolly."

"Aw, baby. I didn't mean it like that. She'll be fine." He came and sat next to her on the bed. "And so will you. Don't worry. I'm sure it'll be over before you know it." He gave her a light kiss. "I've got to run home and change. It seems a few buttons are missing from my shirt." He grinned seductively. "I'm due in court at nine and I have meet to Percy at noon."

She pressed her lips together and nodded. Chase kissed her again. "I love you, sweetie. Remember that."

"I know. I love you, too."

He stood. "Call me as soon as you can."

"I will."

"And, Miki, you've got to remember that there are going to be things that will come up during the course of this investigation and possible trial, that I'm not going to be able to discuss with you. You have to be prepared for that." He held her chin for a moment. "Good luck, and call me." He grabbed his jacket from the back of the chair and walked out.

Michelene slowly got up from the bed, padding into the bathroom and hoped that the soothing beat of the water would ease the tension that knotted her body.

When Percy opened the door to his house, Chase barely missed knocking him down as he pushed passed him.

"Hey, what the—"

Chase spun toward him, his face a mask of contained fury. "Shut up! Don't you say a damn word unless it's the truth. You got me."

Percy shut the door. "Listen, you can't just come in here—"

"How long did you think it was going to take before the police—somebody, put you and Lisa together? Huh? How long did you think you could bullshit me, Percy? This isn't going to just blow over like a shooting slump. We're talking about your life."

Percy's face flushed crimson. Thoughtfully, he walked passed Chase, crossed the living room to the bar and fixed himself a bourbon—straight.

Chase dropped his briefcase next to the couch. "Now do you want to tell me what really happened—what was really going on with you and Lisa Renoir?"

Chase took a seat on the couch, crossed his right ankle over his left knee, and waited. He didn't care if it took all night. Percy Hawkins was going to tell all. The only thing that tugged on his thoughts like bait on a hook was the grilling Michelene was sure to be getting at police headquarters. That, and the hope that the full coroner's report would be on his desk

140

when he returned to his office.

Percy took a long, slow swallow of his drink, trying to frame the words in his head that would somehow begin to explain his relationship and feelings for Lisa.

How could he tell this black man that he'd been raised in a world where black women were considered no more than pieces of property, an easy lay? They'd rock your world in bed, but you didn't bring them home, you didn't take them out in public and you damn sure didn't fall in love with them. How could he say that and withstand the disgust he was sure to see on Chase's face, the same disgust he felt in the bottom of his stomach, but had never been strong enough to get rid of?

"Are you going to talk to me, or keep sipping that drink until you're drunk?"

Percy took another swallow to fortify himself before crossing the room and sitting opposite Chase on the leather recliner.

"I've known Lisa for about two years," he began softly. "I sort of wandered in her gallery one day and there she was, studying a piece of sculpture like it was the most important thing in the world."

A short smile softened the taut lines around Percy's mouth. "The first thing I thought when I saw her was, I wish she'd look at me with the same kind of loving intensity."

Percy shook his head as if his own revelation baffled him. "I don't know where the thought came from, you know. But all of a sudden it was there and I couldn't get rid of it. Then it was as if she read my mind. She looked up and her eyes focused right on me as if I was the only person in the room. Man, when she smiled, my insides went crazy," Percy confessed, reliving the moment.

"Hi. Can I help you?" Lisa smiled and came from around the other side of the blue veined marble table that supported the statue.

"I'm Lisa Renoir, owner of The Gallery," she said, extending her hand to Percy.

"Percy Hawkins."

"I know. I've seen your picture."

"Ever see a game?" Percy asked.

"Not a live one."

"Maybe we could change that."

Her right eyebrow arched. "Really. How's that?"

"I'll see that you get tickets to whatever game you want. Provided I'm playing."

They both laughed.

"Why?" Lisa asked sobering.

Percy looked at her for a moment. "Because I like your smile."

Lisa lowered her gaze, suddenly feeling awkward and nervous.

"Hey, I'm sorry. I didn't mean to embarrass you," he apologized.

Lisa looked around The Gallery, folded her arms beneath her breasts, then focused back on Percy.

"I appreciate the offer, but I couldn't."

His smile wobbled. "No problem." He blew out a breath. "Tell me a little about this picture over here." He pointed to a Jean Michel Basquiat.

"It's an original. Painted shortly before he died."

"How much is it?"

"Seventy-five thousand dollars."

Percy turned to her and whistled. "For that? It's just blobs of paint tossed across the canvas."

She laughed. "It's what you see in the blobs that counts, the passion that the artist exudes in the piece."

"You're kidding, right?"

Lisa bit back a smile. "No."

Percy slung his hands in his pockets and stared at her. "Do you think it's worth it?"

"It depends on what you like," she said tactfully. "It depends on what fulfills your sensibilities. To some, this piece is priceless. To others they will never see the genius behind the work. To each his own as they say."

"Would you hang it on your wall?"

She gazed up at him, her expression questioning. *"Why do you ask?"*

"Just wondering if you're the type of woman who can see the passion and genius behind the work—enough to hang it in your house."

"If I could afford it, I would. I think it's masterful. One of his best."

"Show me some others—please."

Lisa showed him around The Gallery, pointing out and explaining the different pieces of art, from abstract Picasso to Grenadian-born artist Denzil Forrester's *Red Room*. There were rare photographs by Gordon Parks and Franklyn Rodgers, whose experimental photography, which manipulates shadows, and juxtapositions of apparently dissimilar objects with the human form, was portrayed in *Monolith*, a choice example of his investigation of the unexpected. Or at least that's what Percy was told by Lisa. He didn't have a clue, but he liked listening to the sound of her voice and the authoritative matter in which she described the pieces.

Before he knew it, he'd been wandering around listening to the melodic sound of her voice for more than an hour.

"Hey, I've taken up enough of your time," Percy said. *"But I learned a lot."*

She smiled. *"It was my pleasure."*

"You take checks?"

"Sure." Her eyes widened. *"Is there something you've decided on?"*

"Yes. Do you deliver?"

"Of course."

"Personally?"

She got that uncomfortable look on her face again. *"We use a delivery service."*

"If I pay for something now, how long before delivery?"

"I can have it to you tomorrow."

"In that case, I'll take the Basquiat."

"You will?" she asked, her voice rising in pitch.

He chuckled. *"You convinced me that it's great. So it must be. I'll take your word for it."*

"I...don't know what to say."

"Maybe you could ask me for my address."

Percy took a breath and looked across at Chase. "That's how it started. Whenever I was in town, I'd stop in to see her. We'd talk. I'd call her when I was away. We never discussed the fact that we never went out together, or that she never met any of my friends and I never met any of hers. It was...understood...somehow." He shrugged, clasping his hands in front of him.

"Where did the two of you meet...to talk?" Chase asked, trying to keep the sting out of his voice.

"When I was in town, I'd usually go to her place. It's out near the bayou, and..."

"None of your friends would think to find you there?"

Percy's face grimaced in humiliation. He looked away. "You don't understand," he mumbled. "What I was feeling for Lisa went against everything I'd been taught. Everything. It was tearing me up inside."

"But not enough for you to stand up against all of the prejudice," Chase spat, knowing that he had to remain unbiased. But he couldn't help the loathing he was beginning to feel.

Percy's eyes flashed. "It's not that easy."

Chase momentarily looked away in disgust. "Go on," he said from between his teeth.

"Lisa understood the situation. She never made any demands on me. I promised her I'd try to work it out. Find a way for us to really be together."

"But what happened, Percy? Lisa began putting too much pressure on you? Did she threaten to tell all, and you got pissed and killed her? Did you?"

"No!" He sprang up from his seat. "It wasn't like that!" Percy began pacing. "Oh, God," he moaned on a strangled sob. "We fought that night. I didn't mean to hurt her. Oh, God," he collapsed in the chair, covered his face with his hands and wept.

Chase's pulse raced. Had he heard right? Did Percy

144

Hawkins just admit to killing Lisa Renoir?

"Percy. Percy," Chase said in a low, urgent voice, jarring Percy from his flight from reality. "Talk to me, Percy. What happened that night? You've got to come clean so I can help you."

When Percy looked up, his blue eyes were watery and red-rimmed. It appeared as though he'd aged ten years in a matter of minutes. He sniffed loudly and ran a hand through his hair.

"What did you fight about?"

"She'd called me in Chicago. She said we needed to talk as soon as possible. It was important. I told her I wouldn't be back to Louisiana for at least six weeks. I was in training and I couldn't get away."

Percy stared off into space, the phone conversation as clear as daylight in his mind.

"Fine," Lisa said, her voice tremulous as she fought to hold back tears. "I'll work it out myself."

"Work what out? Why can't you tell me over the phone?"

"Forget it, Percy. I should have known better than to get involved with you in the first damn place!" She slammed down the phone and didn't call back.

Percy took a breath and looked at Chase. "Every time I tried to reach her, I'd get her machine at home, or one of her assistants at The Gallery. It was making me nuts, but there wasn't anything I could do.

"When I did get back, I went straight to her house the first chance I got. She wouldn't let me in. Told me to go to hell. That I'd ruined her life." Percy shook his head as the horror of that night came rushing back.

"I'm not leaving here until you tell me what the hell is going on, Lisa."

"Go 'head, yell, Percy Hawkins. Let everybody know you're sneaking around with a coon." She was crying so hard, the words tumbled out in bursts of starts and stops. "Isn't that what y'all call us behind our back? I don't mean any more to you than a quick fix and you're on your way."

"Lisa, please. Let me in. It's not like that. Please. Lisa.

I...love you. You know that."

It seemed like an eternity, but by degrees the door cracked open and Lisa peered out, her eyes swollen from crying, her hair in disarray, her makeup smeared. Percy got scared. He'd never seen Lisa like this. She was always cool and in control. It was one of the things he liked about her—she could handle herself.

Percy stepped in and quickly shut the door behind him. Lisa turned away and walked further into the house, moving through the space like a ghost. His anxiety mounted.

He followed her into the living room. She flopped down into an armchair.

"Lisa what is going on?"

She looked up at him with hopelessness in her eyes. "I...I'm in trouble, Percy."

Percy's heart banged in his chest. He feared the worst. "What kind of trouble? What are you talking about?"

As Chase listened, his fears mounting with the retelling, other things began to fall into place like poker chips on a winning hand. Now it all was beginning to make sense.

Percy and Chase stared at each other. "I pushed her. Hard. I know I did," Percy said, his voice shaking like a leaf. "She banged her head against the marble fireplace and fell to the floor. I tried to wake her. But she wouldn't open her eyes. I panicked. She was alive, I swear she was. So I left. I shut the door and I drove home."

Chase could win this case if it went to trial after all, he realized. But unless he came up with another suspect, the railroad to the courthouse was heading their way.

Chase exhaled a long breath. There was one piece of evidence that had been confirmed early on about Lisa's murder, not released to the public, only revealed to the D.A. and defense counsel. "I know you didn't kill Lisa Renoir, Percy. She didn't die from a blow to the head. Lisa was strangled. So if you didn't kill her, someone else did."

—◄◈►—

New Orleans Police Department

"How long did you know Ms. Renoir, Ms. Tyner?" Detective Thoreau asked, tapping his pen against the scarred metal desktop.

Michelene looked at Pamela who nodded her head.

"Since we were kids. We grew up on the same street. I told you all this before."

"Yes, you did, didn't you. Maybe this long-time friendship was the reason she left you so secure financially."

"I didn't know anything about the money until Lisa's attorney told me."

"But you must admit that this windfall will set you straight for life."

"You don't have to respond to that," Pamela Mitchell advised. "What is your point?" she asked, directing her question to Detectives Paz and Thoreau.

'The point, Ms. Mitchell," replied Paz, "is that your client had an awful lot to gain by Ms. Renoir's death."

"What!" Michelene jumped from her seat. "How dare you. You filthy bastards! Lisa was my friend." Her voice broke "My best friend. The only family I had." Her eyes burned, threatening to tear, but she wouldn't break down. She couldn't believe what she was hearing. They were insinuating that she had something to do with Lisa's death. She started to tremble with rage.

"Michelene," Pamela hissed, grabbing her arm. "Calm down." She glared at the detectives. "Is there something of substance you wish to ask my client, Detectives?"

"What was your financial situation before Ms. Renoir's death?" Paz asked.

"I'm sure you have your ways of finding out," Michelene spat, totally unnerved and completely incensed.

"Of course we do. But if you answer the question, it would make our jobs that much easier."

"And why would I want to do that?" Michelene snapped.

"As you said, Ms. Renoir was your dear friend. I would

think you'd want to cooperate so we could clear this up as quickly as possible," Thoreau said, dragging out every word until they almost blended together. "You do want the case resolved, don't you, Ms. Tyner?"

"Of course I do." Slowly she stood, placed her hands, palms down on the metal table. "However, I'm not going to be railroaded into anything. If you have something specific to ask, then ask it. If not, I'm leaving."

"Is my client under arrest, gentlemen?" Pamela asked, casually shoving her legal pad into her briefcase. She gazed up at them before standing.

"No," Paz answered.

"Then we'll be going. And the next time you go on a fishing expedition, gentlemen, use better bait."

Michelene turned without another word and walked out, followed by Pamela. By the time she reached the stairs to walk down the one flight to the street, her knees were shaking so bad she thought they'd give out.

"You were great in there," Pamela said when they'd cleared the threshold of the precinct and stood on the street.

Michelene spun toward her, eyes blazing. "Did you hear what they said in there?" she demanded, her voice an octave above normal. "They were trying to implicate me somehow—that I had something to do with Lisa's death."

"Take it easy, Miki," Pamela soothed. "They were just going through the motions. It's common practice to look at anyone who may benefit from another's death as a suspect."

"Suspect!"

"Yes. And as hard as it is for you to swallow, what happened to Lisa worked in your favor."

"I don't give a damn about the money or The Gallery or the house or any other material things of hers for that matter."

"What it is you feel and how it looks to an outsider are two different things, Michelene. That's reality. But as I said, you don't have anything to worry about."

Michelene blew out a frustrated breath. "How many others will think I had something to do with this?"

Pamela shrugged. "There'll always be talk. You know that." She paused a moment. "I didn't want to bring this up before, especially not in there, but your portfolio is not what it was. When you didn't take my advice a few months ago and sell, you lost a great deal of money."

"What are you saying?"

"I'm saying that eventually the police may look at that as a motive."

Michelene gave Pamela a long look of disdain, turned and walked down the street toward her car.

Fortunately Michelene hadn't made any appointments for the day. She wouldn't have been any good to her clients if she had. And how many clients would she have after the smoke cleared? What if some of her clients thought the same thing the police did about her?

She stretched out across her bed, staring up at the ceiling. What would she do? Most of her adult life she'd prided herself on her intuitive ability to know and understand people. But it appeared as if the skill, which had been her bread and butter, had totally abandoned her.

Michelene looked around the room, hoping that the soothing colors of the space would work their magic. They didn't.

She shut her eyes, knowing that she should call Chase and let him know she was all right, but she didn't have the energy. She was completely drained.

Dreams—some vague some vivid—swirled in her head, making her toss in her sleep. But as the pictures and voices came into focus, the past few weeks marched before her eyes like trained soldiers. Everything she needed to know was right in front of her.

Suddenly, she sprung up from her sleep, her eyes wide open. Tossing aside the sheet, she hurried, barefoot, downstairs and went straight to her office. She pulled open the file cabinet drawer and removed the folder of photocopies and took it to her desk. She retrieved her palm top from her bag and turned it on along with her PC.

Within moments she was comparing the entries in the computer to the documents in the folder. With each comparison her heart raced faster and the lead weight of dread grew heavier in her stomach.

Chase returned to DuBois, Merchant and Alexander, breezed by Marie and shut the door to his office. As he'd hoped, the sealed coroner's report was on his desk. He ripped the envelope open and quickly scanned the contents. "Just as I thought," he mumbled. He picked up the phone and dialed.

"District Attorney Dunham's office."

"Chase Alexander. Is Anthony around?"

"He has someone in his office, Mr. Alexander. Can I take a message?"

Chase blew out a breath of frustration. "Please have him call me at my office. It's urgent." He gave her his office number.

"Of course."

Chase hung up the phone and read the documents again. This time, slower. He shook his head in sad acceptance, closing the folder. *What could be worse than being betrayed by someone you trust?* he mused.

Chapter Fourteen

The Best Laid Plans

Michelene methodically collected all of the papers and put them back into the folder. There was no point in getting rid of the copies of the airline tickets, since she'd been foolish enough to turn them over to Anthony.

She stuck the file back in the cabinet and locked it. What Anthony didn't have were the receipts. There were hundreds of them, going back over the previous year. At least she'd had the good sense to hold on to those until she had a chance to look through them, see what they really meant. Trouble.

Ooh, she could kick herself for being so self-righteous. She'd been so hell-bent on proving Chase wrong, and hanging Percy in the process that she hadn't thought things through before calling Anthony.

But that was water under the bridge. There was nothing she could do about it now. She needed to deal with the problem at hand. Sighing, she turned off her computer. This was much bigger than she'd ever imagined. What to do?

Lisa was her friend and no matter who or what she was involved with or in, she wanted to protect her name and her reputation. At the very least, for Lisa's mother's sake. She didn't think Ms. Renoir could handle much more. Whatever she already knew about her daughter had been enough to crush what was left of her spirit.

But maybe Ms. Renoir could tell her something that would make sense. Maybe these pieces she was putting together were all in the wrong place. Silently she prayed they were.

Deciding not to take a chance on being turned down by Ms. Renoir, Michelene made up her mind to pay a visit. Hopefully there was something Ms. Renoir could tell her that would make the impending feeling of dread go away. And until it did, she wouldn't share what she'd discovered with anyone.

At the knocking on the office door, Chase looked up from the documents on his desk.

"It's open."

Lance walked in.

"I was getting ready to buzz you," Chase said, pushing his seat a bit away from the desk.

"That the coroner's report?" Lance asked with a lift of his chin in the direction of the papers on the desk.

"Yeah. It was here when I got back."

"Can I see it?"

"Sure." Chase pushed the folder across the desk.

Lance picked it up and sat down, thumbing through the file. "So how do things stand with the case?" he asked without looking up.

"Unfortunately all roads lead back to our hero," Chase said. "He did finally admit to me that he knew Lisa and was sleeping with her."

Lance glanced up. "That changes things."

"And according to that file, he had motive."

"What do you plan to do?"

"I'm sure Anthony is going to move to indict based on the evidence," Chase said.

"Looks like we're going to trial then."

"I have a few leads that I'm checking out." He gazed down at his hands for a moment then across to Lance, giving him a quarter of a smile. "You know Michelene and Lisa were best friends."

"And..."

"A little pillow talk." He shrugged. "Never know what I may find out. She's been very helpful so far."

Lance smiled. "So you got her to come around I take it."

"Of course."

Lance shook his head in amazement. "I knew you were the one to handle this case. If anyone can get Percy Hawkins off it's you." He stood, tucking the file under his arm. "Keep me posted. I want to take a closer look at this file. I'll get it right back to you."

"Take your time. I've seen all I need to see."

Lance nodded and walked out.

Chase stared at the door for a very long time after Lance's departure.

"Who is it?" came a threadbare voice from the other side of the closed door.

"Mrs. Renoir, it's me, Michelene. I need to talk to you."

Slowly the door was pulled open. Wide, sad eyes peered back at Michelene. "If it's anything about Lisa, I really don't want to talk, Michelene," Mrs. Renoir said.

"Please, you may be the only one who can answer my questions. I need to know what was going on with Lisa. I have my suspicions but I think you know much more than I do."

Celeste shook her head. "Let it rest, Michelene."

"I can't. And neither should you."

"Exposing everything won't bring her back."

"I know." She blew out a breath. "Maybe you're right. It's just that Lisa was my friend, or at least I thought she was. But suddenly I don't know who she was."

Celeste looked at her for a moment, then stepped aside. "Come in," she said softly.

When Michelene left Celeste Renoir's home two hours

later, she had the answers she needed, but she felt no better about knowing that her suspicions were true. Driving home, she tried to clear her head. Should she go to Anthony with the information she had, or should she give it to Chase?

No matter which way she sliced it, Chase was defending the man who was responsible for Lisa's death, whether he wanted to accept that fact or not. What complicated matters further was that this went way beyond Percy Hawkins. How far, she was still uncertain.

━━◆◆◆━━

Lance scrutinized every letter contained in the coroner's report. He didn't like what he saw. Not at all. When he told Percy that Chase could get him out of this mess, he had no idea of what would turn up. Percy had lied to him. He didn't take that lightly. He had too much at stake for some hick kid who made good to blow it for him by being stupid.

Lance looked at the papers again. And this was stupid. How much had Lisa confided in Michelene?

━━◆◆◆━━

At least now he had a plan, Chase thought as he packed up for the evening. If he could convince Michelene to cooperate, everything might just work out with the least amount of damage. A lot of folks were going down behind this and he'd be more than happy to see it happen.

The phone rang. He hoped it was Anthony, there was no way he could pull this off without the D.A.'s help.

"Hello? Yeah, Tony. We need to talk. It's about the Hawkins case. Yeah, I know we're not on the same team, but there are some things you need to know and I need your help. Yes, it is. Where can we meet? Perfect. See you there in about twenty minutes."

Chase hung up and headed for the door. This has to work.

When Chase arrived at The Place, he spotted Anthony who was already seated at a table in the back. Anthony was deep in conversation with Kenny when he approached.

Kenny stood. "Long time." He stuck out his hand, which Chase shook. "I'll leave you two alone."

"No, stay. I want you to tell Chase what you told me," Tony instructed.

"I think I already know," Chase said taking a seat. "But I'd still like to hear it from you."

Reluctantly, Kenny sat back down. "Where do you want me to start?"

"When did the meetings begin?" Chase asked.

Kenny shrugged. "About eight, nine months ago. I didn't pay it much attention at first. But I've been in this business a long time. And one thing I know about The Place, no one ever comes here just once. But this parade of stars certainly did."

"How many would you say passed through here," Tony quizzed.

"At least a half dozen."

"Was Lisa Renoir ever in on these meetings?" Tony asked.

"I never saw her sit in on any, but she was around a few times when they took place. What does all of this have to do with Lisa's death?"

"What about Michelene?" Chase asked, holding his breath. "Was she ever in on the meetings?"

He shook his head. "Not that I've ever seen. You're not trying to involve her in any of this, are you?" he asked, his voice and face hardening.

"Michelene's already involved," Chase said. "More than that I can't tell you."

Kenny clenched his jaw, then pointed his finger at Chase. "Let me tell you something, Mr. New York Lawyer, Michelene Tyner is a decent person. Sure she flirts and wiggles her way in and out of things, but something like this—never. Don't even think about dragging her into it," he warned.

"Take it easy, Kenny," Tony said, catching Kenny's arm. "We're all on the same side here."

"Are we? Isn't he the one who's defending a murderer and trying to imply that Michelene is involved?" He stood, nearly knocking over the chair. "You need to be looking at Sylvia Tanner. She was always in here." He turned and walked away.

Tony blew out a breath. "I guess you know Kenny's been in love with Michelene damn near all his life. He's a bit over-protective."

Chase looked away. "I kind of got that. Why did the two of you break it off?" he asked, catching Tony off guard.

"She told you—about us?"

"No. She didn't have to. I spend a lot of my time investigating, Tony. When I got involved with Michelene I found out the two of you had been seeing each other. That was easy enough to do. Sylvia Tanner was more than happy to tell me about you and Michelene. But I never discussed it with Michelene. I guess that's one of the reasons she felt she could come to you with information. Because you had history."

"Let's just say things didn't work out and we decided it was best we go our separate ways. There were some—issues that we didn't see eye-to-eye on. I will say this, though, and only because you're my friend and I know you care about her. Nothing ever happened. She wouldn't let it."

"Knowing you like I do, Tony, I can only imagine. But thanks for saying that. So, what do you have on Sylvia?"

"Not much. But I have a feeling you do." Tony's said, relieved to have gotten off the tender topic. He was forever sorry that things didn't work out between him and Michelene, but there was that dark side of him that few women could handle. He always believed it was what made him such a ruthless prosecutor, a way to express the rage he sometimes felt.

Chase relayed his conversation with Sylvia and his plan to use Michelene if she was willing.

"Do you think you can get Miki to agree?" Tony asked.

"I know she wants to get to the truth as much as you and I."

Tony nodded. "I'll put everything in place. I just hope it works."

"It will. I can guarantee it."

Tony looked at his long time friend. "We've been on opposite sides of the fence for so long, buddy. It's good we're finally on the same team."

"Hey, I'd do just about anything not to have to face you in the courtroom," Chase said with a smile.

"I think it would have been fun. Give me a chance to see what you really have." He took a sip of his drink.

"Believe me, you wouldn't want to do that."

They eyed each other.

"To challenges," Tony said, raising his glass in a toast.

"To justice," Chase countered.

Chapter Fifteen

All Good Things

When Michelene returned to her town house, twilight was settling over the city. The sky was beginning to fill with stars and the moon hung at a precarious angle. A gentle, but muggy breeze blew off the Mississippi. The oak trees swayed as if doing a slow dance to unheard music.

All around her, life tiptoed in the rustle of grass, the crackle of leaves, the soaring of birds and the ripple of water that flowed in the stream behind her house. It appeared that all was well and beautiful with the world.

It wasn't.

Weary, Michelene turned the key in the lock and went inside. She needed to call Chase. She'd made up her mind on the drive. She'd turn over what information she had and let him do with it what needed to be done. She just wanted it all to be over.

"Lisa, Lisa why?" she called out to the empty space. Placing her purse on the hall table, she went to her office to check her messages. She pressed the flashing red button.

"Michelene, it's Chase. When you get in, please stay put. I'll be over. We need to talk."

Her stomach knotted in tension. Did he have more fuel to add to the fire? She could tell by his tone that he didn't want to declare his undying love. So it couldn't be good news.

Michelene went upstairs with the intention of washing away the grit of hurt that covered her skin and seeped into her pores.

She still hadn't told Mrs. Renoir about her inheritance from Lisa, although with everything else that Celeste Renoir had discovered about her daughter, she probably knew that as well.

When this mess was finally straightened out, she would have everything turned over to Lisa's mother, she decided, lathering her body with peach-scented soap. She didn't need the money and she didn't want it. Maybe Mrs. Renoir could find a way to put it to good use. She'd let Pamela take care of the particulars.

Turning off the water, Michelene wrapped herself in a thick towel and headed for her bedroom. Sitting in front of her dressing table mirror, she wondered again what it was Chase wanted to talk with her about. He didn't say what time he would arrive, but she wanted to be prepared when he did.

She slipped on a pale blue satin lounging outfit and went downstairs. Usually she didn't drink, especially when she was alone. But tonight she felt as if she needed one. Just as she finished pouring a short glass of wine, the bell rang.

"Chase," she whispered and her pulse rushed with anticipation and dread.

"Who is it?" she asked at the door.

"It's Lance."

She frowned, trying to search her mind, thinking maybe she'd made an appointment with him and had forgotten.

Opening the door, she put on her best smile even though what she really felt was disappointment. Lance was really sweet, but he wasn't who she wanted to see at the moment.

"Lance. Hi, honey. What brings you around here?"

"I just had you on my mind, sugah, and I wanted to check for myself and see how you were."

She leaned against the door frame, knowing that once she let him in, there was no telling how long he would wind up staying. Lance did like to chat.

"Not too bad, considering. I'm working again. Can't afford to lose my clients."

"Good. Glad to hear that." He looked over her shoulder.

"But even if you did, I understand you now have a sizable amount of money that Lisa left you."

"How did you know that?"

"I have friends at police headquarters. People talk."

She didn't reply.

"But I wouldn't worry about it."

"Worry about what?"

"Talk. Rumors. That sort of thing."

She swallowed. "I'll keep that in mind. Listen, Lance, I would invite you in but I'm expecting Chase any minute now."

"Sure. I didn't mean to take up your time. I just wanted to know you were all right. You know you're one of my favorite people. Chase is a lucky man. I'm glad things worked out between the two of us. I mean...with Lisa, the case and everything."

She smiled. "Thanks."

"I'd better go, then. Tell you what, why don't we get together when I get back? Maybe have dinner or something."

"I'd like that. Where are you heading to now?"

"New York. Just for a couple of days. I'm leaving tomorrow night. I have a new client out there that's ready to do some business overseas."

"You keep reeling them in," she said with a smile.

"We all have to be good at something." He leaned down and kissed her cheek. "Take care, sugah. We'll talk. And, Michelene, please don't think badly of me because the firm took on Percy's case. I've known Percy for years, and as much as I cared about Lisa and feel horrible about what happened, I still believe that Percy deserves the best representation. And Chase happens to be it."

"I understand," she said.

He nodded. "So long as there's no hard feelings." He turned to go.

"Thanks for stopping by, Lance."

He waved and headed to his car. Michelene stood in the doorway and watched him drive away before closing the door.

That was nice, she thought, returning to the living room,

even though the tail end of the conversation stirred up things she'd rather not think about. She sat on the couch and pointed the remote at the television, and began surfing, trying to let her mind wander and relax. She leaned back against the cushions and shut her eyes. The conversation with Lisa's mother and the scene at her house, floated back in waves...

"Did you look in the envelope before you gave it to me at Lisa's house, Mrs. Renoir? The one that was inside the box?"

Celeste turned away. She couldn't look Michelene in the eye. "I brought the envelope with me and put it in the box."

"What? Those were your receipts?"

Slowly she shook her head. "No. They belonged to Lisa."

"Why did you have them, and why did you give them to me?"

Celeste pressed her trembling lips together. Her eyes began to fill. "I...told Lisa what she was doing was wrong. She wouldn't listen."

"What was she doing, Mrs. Renoir?" She had a good idea, but she needed Celeste to confirm her worst fears.

"For that...man," she sobbed, covering her face with her hands.

"Percy? Percy Hawkins?"

The doorbell rang. Michelene's eyes flew open. Shaking her head to clear it, she slowly stood and went to the door. "Coming."

"It's Chase, Michelene."

She exhaled a sigh of relief and pulled the door open, walking straight into his arms. "Chase," she whispered against his chest. "I'm glad you're here. I have so much to tell you."

"So do I," he said, hugging her tight.

"Come on inside."

—◆—

Michelene was stunned by what Chase told her, compounded with what Lisa's mother had added, it made her head spin.

"How could this have happened, Chase?" she said, agonized over what Lisa had allowed herself to become enmeshed in.

"Greed, love, jealousy," he said, plainly. "But until they show their hand we really can't prove anything. I don't want anyone getting off on some technicality."

Michelene nodded.

"So I need your help."

"Me? What can I do?"

"I want to use you as bait. Word is out about the money you got from Lisa. And I'm sure they think you have information that could bring the whole thing down."

"The receipts?"

"Yes. The receipts prove the transactions of the stolen merchandise and connect to the trips, and all the data that you collected on your palm top; appointments, whereabouts of clients, all that. It may have seemed like a matter of course to you at the time, just trying to be efficient, but it's crucial. It's all pieces of the same puzzle."

Michelene wrapped her arms around her waist and curled her legs beneath her on the couch. "Whatever it takes," she said. She turned to look at him. "Whatever."

Chase stroked her hair. "I can't begin to imagine how difficult this must be on you, Miki."

"I only wish I knew how unhappy and lonely Lisa really was, Chase. Maybe I could have helped. But over the months she started shutting herself away from me, becoming secretive. Now I know why," she said sadly.

"Love is a very powerful thing, Michelene. And when it gets twisted out of control, there's no telling what someone will do for it or to have it."

"But she was such a wonderful person. She could have had anyone she wanted. She didn't need to go to the lengths she did to prove she was worthy of Percy's love, anyone's love. My God."

"Sometimes you think you know someone. You can spend your life with them and still never know all of the dark spaces in their hearts."

"I'm beginning to finally understand that. Too much of what I took as being who a person was were the things they liked, their personal tastes, the amount of money they had, the cars they drove. Sure it may be a part of who they are, but it's definitely not everything. And even as close as Lisa and I were, she was never able to share with me the hurt that was going on inside of her. Her feelings of inadequacy."

"Maybe she believed you'd think less of her, Michelene. Look at you. You have it all. A great business, you're beautiful, everyone loves you and you have the ability to twist people around on your little finger. You have men dropping at your feet. You exude confidence, Michelene. It can be intimidating to someone with less self-assurance."

She snuggled closer to Chase. "Thinking about it now, perhaps that was the reason why Lisa kept herself hidden away in The Gallery. She felt safe there. It was where she was in control." Dispirited, she shook her head. "When she did venture out, she eventually got herself killed. I should have been paying more attention. I should have known, Chase. Here I am, running around bragging about how much I know about people, and I didn't know a damn thing about my best friend."

Chase wrapped his arm around her and kissed the top of her head. "Don't do this to yourself, Miki. You didn't know because Lisa didn't want you to know. It's as simple as that."

She looked up into his eyes. "You really think so?"

"Yeah. I do. You couldn't have prevented this."

Michelene sighed. "I don't ever want what we feel for each other to destroy us, Chase. This is the first time in my life that I actually feel safe and secure with a man. I don't have to pretend it's wonderful, because it actually is."

"Baby, whatever it takes to make this work between us I'm willing to try." His eyes roamed her face. "You've changed me. That hard core that was my center has softened. I was never good at relationships, my career was more important. It was the only thing that mattered. Until you. And I'm going to do everything I can to keep you safe so we can move on with our lives and build a future together."

Michelene stroked his cheek, easing closer until her lips touched his. "I love you, Chase," she whispered against his mouth. "And I'm scared."

"I'm going to protect you, Miki. Believe that," he said, covering her mouth with his. "There's no way I'm going to risk losing you."

Their mouths became one single note on the scale. Perfect. Their bodies drew closer, flowing along the curves and contours like the Mississippi moving along its banks. They fit.

Chase's hands glided along the satiny fabric, caressing the supple flesh beneath. He heard her sighs, felt her body tremble as he took his time reacquainting himself with her exquisite body. His fingers inched under the hem of her top, crept along the hollow of her stomach, upward until he felt the tender underside of her breasts.

"Chase," she gasped, clutching his hand, pressing it closer to her breasts. "I've missed you terribly."

"I'm more than happy," he whispered, "to make up for lost time."

His tongue slid across her mouth, just enough to tingle, to taste, before slipping between her lips, even as he eased the satin pants down her legs, exposing her bare, smooth flesh.

Michelene caressed his back, feeling the pulse of his muscles move beneath her fingertips as his body began to move against hers. She tried to concentrate on just making him feel good, letting him know that he was loved, but when his fingers eased between the folds of her sex and her entire body contracted then released in a sudden spasm of delight, all reason flew from her head.

Her nimble fingers found their way between pressed flesh to unloosen Chase's clothing, nearly ripping it in the process.

"You ever think this sense of urgency, this frenzy...to be with each other will ever end?" Michelene asked, breathless and trembling as she felt Chase's nakedness fully against hers.

Chase looked down at her, his eyes dark, smoldering with raw need. The corner of his mouth curved. "No, baby. I want to be loving you..." He pressed against her opening. "Like this..." He eased in a little further and her eyes drifted shut, her breath caught. "For as long as you let me."

And then he was there, all of him, surrounded by her heat, and a strangled cry rose from his throat. Her hips moved in slow, tantalizing motion—taunting and teasing him, the muscles drawing him in, letting him go.

Heaven. This was heaven on earth, Chase thought, turning his body over to the total joy of their union. Never before had he felt like this with a woman. He'd never allowed himself to be this vulnerable to his emotions. But with Michelene he couldn't help himself.

He held her tighter, wishing he could absorb her under his skin, silently praying that he would be able to protect and keep her safe—with him for always.

"I love you, Michelene," he uttered on a ragged breath, the power of their loving racing through him in electric waves.

"I love you, Chase," she moaned, his movements within her body leaving her weak, wanting and strong all at once. Every nerve ending in her body was alive, on fire. The sensations were almost too much to withstand, but she didn't want them to ever end. To go on forever, with these feelings rippling through her, holding her man against her...yeah, she could live with that...

"How do you know this is going to work?" Michelene asked as they spooned in her bed. She was beginning to get jumpy again.

Chase kissed the back of her neck. "I don't. I just know we have to try. They're going to come after you, Michelene. If not now, when we go to trial. There's too much at stake. I want to be prepared, set the ground rules on my terms. I don't want any surprises."

"Where will this all leave Percy when it's over?"

"I'm sure we'll be able to work out a deal with Anthony."

He felt her body tighten. He stroked her arm, kissed her shoulder. "What ever happened with you and Anthony?" he gently asked.

She shrugged. "It didn't work out. At one point I really thought he might be 'the one.' He was handsome, successful, put on a good show. All the things that catch your eye. But underneath the great exterior..." She shuddered. "There's a side to Tony that I didn't want to be a part of. And we both realized that before things got out of hand."

"Hmm."

"I guess he told you, huh?" she asked.

"No, not really. It was Sylvia."

Michelene laughed. "How ironic."

"None of that matters—whatever we did before each other. Now is what counts."

"You're right." She paused a moment. "When do you think it's going to happen, Chase? When are they going to come after me?"

He tightened his arm around her, drawing her closer. "Within the next few days."

She swallowed. "How do you know?"

"Because I'm going to make sure that they do."

Chapter Sixteen

And Then There Were None

"I have someone staking out her place," Anthony said into the phone.

"I don't want anything going wrong, Tony," Chase warned. "Michelene means too much to me."

"Don't worry. Everything's under control. Are you straight on your end?"

"Yeah."

"Good. What about Percy?"

"He knows what he's up against, but as long as he cooperates, I told him we'd work something out."

Anthony chuckled. "We. I guess *we* means *me*. You're not satisfied with your own job, you want to do mine, too. I always said you should have been a prosecutor."

"Not on your life," Chase laughed.

"Take it easy, buddy. And keep me posted."

Chase absently hung up the phone, wondering if he'd done the right thing by getting Michelene so closely involved. But there was no turning back now. He got up from behind his desk and headed for Lance's office.

"Come in," Lance responded to the knock on his door.

"Busy?" Chase asked, stepping in and closing the door.

"Just putting a few things together for this trip. I'm leaving for New York."

"Oh, right. How's that deal looking?"

Lance smiled. "You know me, I'm sure I'll work something out that benefits everyone. This firm in particular."

Chase shoved his hands into his pockets, lowered his head as he paced across the floor. "I need your advice, Lance."

"Sure." He stopped shoving documents in his briefcase and looked at Chase.

"Michelene has a stack of receipts and photocopies of airline tickets and hotel bills that belonged to Lisa."

Lance's brows rose. "Really? Have you...seen them?"

"No. But she seems to think Lisa may have been involved in something illegal along with Percy and maybe others."

"I don't understand. How does she get that from some receipts?"

"You don't know Michelene. She's meticulous to a fault. She keeps records of everything: times, dates, who she saw, what she did, items she purchased and for whom, appointments. You name it, she has a record of it."

"But what does this have to do with Percy's case?"

"It seems as though every date that Michelene has that she and Lisa were supposed to meet, and Lisa either canceled or didn't show up, were the same dates of either these receipts for shipments, or trips out of the state."

A shadow passed across Lance's face. "I see. Did you get them from her? I'm sure the police would be interested."

"Don't you see, if I take them, they might implicate Percy even further."

"Percy?"

"Of course. He's already confessed to having a relationship with Lisa. If the police can connect him to any of these trips, and find a way to tie him to these transactions, the D.A. is going to push for an indictment. There's no two ways about it." He shook his head. "Percy swears to me he didn't kill her. A part of me believes him. But now... I just don't know, Lance. Maybe it was a deal gone sour."

Lance ran a hand across his face. "We obviously can't let the police have the information before we find out exactly what those documents mean." He turned his gaze on Chase. "You need to find a way to convince her to let you take a look at them. It's as simple as that. She can't go to the DA or the police. We need all the ammunition we can to keep Percy out of jail and avoid a trial."

"But what if he's guilty?"

"At this point, does it matter? The firm's reputation is on the line. This is the biggest case this town has seen in decades. I have no intention of walking away from it with my tail between my legs." He picked up his briefcase, came from behind his desk and walked toward the door. "I'm sure you'll have this all straightened out by the time I get back. We'll talk then." He walked out, leaving Chase feeling sick to his stomach.

Michelene paced across the hardwood floors of her bedroom, her shadow dancing across the peach walls. She knew she was safe. There was a detective outside of her house. Somewhere. Chase said so. And she believed him. But it didn't take away the fear that had her heart racing out of control.

She had to stay calm, play it out. She wanted to catch Lance DuBois. She wanted to make him pay for what he'd done to Lisa. And to think he was just at her house. If she'd let him in, she shuddered to think what might have happened.

He'd set the whole thing up. Set Percy up with Lisa. It was Lance's idea for Percy to go to The Gallery and meet Lisa. But he never anticipated that they'd actually fall in love. Lisa was just supposed to be a conduit for his shipment of stolen merchandise in and out of the country. The perfect pawn. Alone, vulnerable and in need of wanting someone to love her.

A sob caught in her throat. If only Lisa would have talked to her, told her what was going on, what she was involved in. Maybe she could have helped her before it was too late. Poor Lisa, thinking that she wasn't good enough for Percy unless she had things, money, a way to be his equal. And Percy was just as responsible for her death as if he'd strangled her himself. Money and greed. Lisa had lost her life for the two deadly sins.

A car was pulling up in her driveway. She hurried to the window and pushed the curtain aside. She couldn't spot the detective. Her hands shook as she held the curtain, peering out into the darkness.

That wasn't Lance's car. Her heartbeat slowed to normal. It was Paul Dupre. *What could he possibly want at this hour? Oh, it must be about Cissy's car.* She'd completely forgotten to get back to him about it.

She went downstairs and was at the door when the bell rang. She pulled the door open, an apology already on her lips.

"Paul. I know you're going to kill me for not getting back to you about the car for Cissy." She smiled warmly and kissed his cheek.

"I sure am. Had me wondering what was going on." He stepped inside. "I know I should have called, but I was out this way and thought I might as well stop by in person." He walked into the foyer and stepped into the living room, turned and faced her. "I was thinking maybe you were upset about Sylvia and I."

"Oh, don't be silly. I'm happy for you. Really."

"You're not expecting company, or anything? I'm not interrupting, am I?"

"Uh, no. Not at all. I was just relaxing. Have a seat. Can I get you something to drink?"

"A beer would be fine, if you have one."

"Sure. Be right back."

Michelene walked into the kitchen and opened the refrigerator, just as she felt a presence move up behind. She spun around and a scream hung in her throat as a hand covered her mouth and pushed her against the wall.

"Where are they?" he hissed, pressing his face within inches of hers.

Her eyes widened as she tried to breathe.

"Don't scream and I'll remove my hand."

Michelene nodded furiously.

Slowly he took his hand away, but slid it down to her

throat. "Now tell me, where are the documents concerning Lisa? I'm not going to ask you again."

"Inside," she gasped, "my office."

"Let's go." He kept his hand around her throat as they walked through the house to the back office.

"Where?" he breathed into her neck when they'd entered the office.

"File cabinet," she choked.

"Open it."

—✦—

Lance put the last of his clothes in his suitcase. He took one more look around, making sure he hadn't forgotten anything, grabbed his suitcase and headed for the door.

When he pulled it open, Percy was standing on the other side.

"What in the hell are you doing here? Are you crazy?"

Percy pushed Lance back inside the house. "You had her killed and you were going to let me take the fall."

Lance stumbled back into the house. "You got it all wrong, Percy. I was trying to help you."

"Help me!" He pulled a .38 from the pocket of his jacket. "She was pregnant, you bastard. With my child!"

Lance held up his hands. "Percy, listen. You're going to beat this thing. Walk away from it clear and with plenty of money."

"I should have never listened to you. I shouldn't have gotten Lisa involved. She did it because she loved me and I used her. I'm no better than you are."

"You did what you wanted to do. You saw an opportunity and you took it. Getting the cash for the stolen art worked out for everyone, me, you, Paul and Lisa. You don't have to do this."

"I don't care if I go to jail for killing you, Lance. I should've been more of a man when Lisa needed me. But I was weak, listening to everything that was wrong. Not anymore."

He cocked the gun.

"Percy. There's more than fifty million dollars in my account overseas. I'll split it with you," he said in a rush.

Percy shook his head. "Not this time, Lance. Money isn't the answer. At least I'll be man enough and get rid of you myself. You had to send Paul to do your dirty work."

"We can work something out," Lance said, backing up and looking frantically around the room. "Don't do this."

"That's what I should have said a long time ago."

The shot threw Lance against the wall, the sound reverberating throughout the house.

Percy let the gun fall to his side and walked to the telephone.

—⋙⟡⋘—

Chase walked back and forth across the floor of his living room. He should have been over there. He shouldn't have left her alone. He checked the time on his watch. According to Marie, Lance's flight was scheduled for 9:00 P.M. It was a little after seven. Whatever he was going to do, it would be soon.

He couldn't stay there and do nothing, no matter how good Anthony said his men on the scene were. He grabbed his jacket just as the phone rang.

"Hello?"

"Chase, it's Anthony. Lance has been shot."

"What? By who?"

"Percy Hawkins. He called the precinct. The police are already there. He's ready to talk. Said it was Paul who killed Lisa and Lance set it up."

Chase momentarily shut his eyes. At least Michelene would be all right. "I'm going over to Michelene's. Let Percy know I'll meet him at the precinct. I think he'll be needing a lawyer."

"Sure. And Chase—"

"Yeah."

"Thanks."

As soon as the call was disconnected, he dialed Michelene's number. The phone rang until the machine picked up. Frowning, Chase hung up. Why wouldn't she answer the phone? Maybe she was in the shower. He headed for the door.

Paul killed Lisa. Lance set it up. "Paul. Oh, my God."

He punched in Anthony's cell phone number. He picked up on the second ring.

"Dunham."

"Tony, has anyone gone into Michelene's house?"

"I didn't get any calls. Hold on. Let me get them on the radio."

Chase listened with dread to the static and muffled voices.

"Chase, I'm sending them in," Anthony said, coming back on the line. "Paul got there about fifteen minutes ago. They were looking for Lance. Man, I'm sorry."

Chase slammed down the phone and raced out the door.

"Please," he prayed, as he raced through the darkening streets. "Don't hurt her."

"I hate that things have to end this way, Michelene. I really loved you," Paul said, snatching the envelope from her hand. "But I worked for twenty years to build my business, I'm not going to lose it because people suddenly got a conscience."

"Is that why you killed Lisa, because she had a conscience?" she asked trying to buy time. "We grew up together, Paul. All three of us."

"And I felt real bad about it too, Michelene." He opened the envelope with his free hand and looked inside. "Lisa knew what she was doing when she would take merchandise that had been transported inside the cars that came to me. She wasn't stupid. She wanted to prove something to lover boy. Between Lisa and Sylvia transferring the goods, we had it made. Until Lisa became Ms. Goody Two Shoes."

"So you're going to kill me, too?" she choked.

"I don't have any choice, cher." His grip tightened around her throat. "You should have let me love you, Michelene," he whispered, his grip cutting off her air.

She started to struggle, going for his face. Paul knocked her to the floor, and pinned her down with his knee, both hands fastened around her neck. "You pick the wrong friends," he said.

Michelene started to feel light-headed. Her arms and legs felt like lead unable to move at her command. Tears sprung to her eyes as she tried to claw his face, wrestle free. She didn't want to die. *Oh, God, please don't let me die.*

Spots danced in front of her eyes, growing bigger until there was nothing in front of her but blackness. Her last thought as she took her final breath was...*Chase.*

Chapter Seventeen

New Beginnings

Lance's funeral was in two hours, and Percy's trial for his murder was scheduled to begin within the next few weeks. Paul's trials for the murder of Lisa and the attempted murder of Michelene would be held separately. Sylvia Tanner agreed to tell all with the promise of immunity. The level of involvement in the illegal shipments and transference of money included some of the most notable figures in Louisiana, from the police department to members of the legislature. Every newspaper across the country ran stories about the biggest scandal in Louisiana history. And it would have worked, except no one gambled on anyone falling in love. One moment in time, a single interlude had ultimately ruined the lives of dozens of people.

Michelene stared into her mirror, stroking the bruises on her neck. It could have been her funeral Chase was about to attend. Another minute, the doctors said, and she wouldn't have made it. It was still hard to swallow and her throat was a bit raw when she talked, but it would all go away in time.

Turning away from the mirror, she crossed the room and took her black dress from the hanger in the closet. A shudder rippled through her every time she thought about that night. If the police and Chase hadn't arrived when they did...She still had nightmares, but the counselor said they too would eventually cease.

Chase eased up behind her, gently caressing her shoulders

before planting a kiss on the back of her neck. "Almost ready?"

Michelene nodded and turned to face him. Her eyes glowed with love when she looked at him. He hadn't left her side since that night.

"You don't have to do this, Miki. No one expects you to be there. There'll be more people there interested in what and who they can see, than because they care one way or the other about Lance DuBois."

"I need to do this," she said in a hoarse whisper. "To put closure to it, so that I can move on. The counselor said I need to face my fears."

He ran his thumb across her bottom lip. "I'll be right by your side the whole time."

"I know." She smiled.

"What do you think made Percy finally snap?" Michelene asked on the ride over to the church.

"According to him, he couldn't live with his conscience any longer and didn't want to see Lance walk away scot-free."

"But you could have gotten Percy off. Everyone could have walked away."

"Yes. There was nothing to directly tie Percy to Lisa's death. But love and conscience are two very powerful things, Miki. Even though Percy went into a rage when Lisa told him about the pregnancy, and that she was getting out of the trafficking business, he never meant to hurt her. He was reacting to old beliefs and deep-rooted fears when he pushed her. Getting rid of Lance, the catalyst for it all, to Percy, was a way to make it up to Lisa. Lance's involvement was international in scope. He used his contacts to move everything. This is going to take a long time to untangle. After they unravel Lisa's finances, there may be something legitimate left over for you to give to her mother."

Michelene slowly shook her head. "Percy lied to me from

the beginning when I asked him about who he was seeing. He said she was married. I guess it was to keep me totally off the track." It was all so horrid and so easily avoidable.

Shortly, the car pulled up in front of the church, and as expected, throngs of reporters, cameramen and gawkers lined the street trying to get a glimpse of any and everyone.

Chase turned to Michelene. "Ready?"

"Yes."

He leaned closer and softly kissed her lips. "I love you."

"I love you, too."

He opened the door, came around the front of the car to her side. Michelene stepped out to a cavalcade of flashbulbs and reporters hurling questions at both her and Chase. Chase put his hand securely around her waist and led her through the crowd to the entrance of the church.

—⋙◈⋘—

One Year Later

"Oh, Mrs. Alexander..."

"Yes, Mr. Alexander," Michelene called from the kitchen of their new home in Atlanta.

"I'm heading over to the university. I have an early class this morning. I think I'll give them a pop quiz," he teased. He eased up behind her wrapping his arms around her swelling belly.

"You're mean. I'm glad I'm not in any of your classes, professor."

"So am I," he said in a low voice. "I wouldn't be able to concentrate if I knew you were sitting there and knowing what we did the night before." He gave her a wicked grin.

"And that's exactly the kind of attitude that has me in this predicament," she taunted, placing his hands on her stomach.

"And I loved every minute of getting you there."

"You better get going before you cause some more trouble, cher."

She walked him to the door. "Chase?"

"Hmm."

"Do you ever regret giving up practicing?"

"No. It was the right decision for me, for us. I couldn't do it anymore, babe. I was losing my sense of ethics, a sense of what was really important. That's why I went into law—to help people. When that stopped happening, it was time for me to go. What about you, darling, any regrets?"

"None," she said, hugging him to her. "The past year has been a real lesson for me. It's not about material things and appearances. But what the person is really about. I let exteriors cloud my judgment and my thinking. Right now all I want to concentrate on is being the best wife and mother I can be."

Chase smiled. "Knowing you, baby, you'll be back at it in no time. You have too much talent and too much energy."

"Well..," she grinned. "I was thinking about opening a small boutique. Nothing fancy. I could have a little playroom in the back for the baby. Maybe even a small café area where the ladies could chat, and..."

Chase tossed his head back and laughed. The years ahead were sure to be full of surprises.